Sister Sunday

A novel

by

Beth Ann Baus

Kathy,
I hope you enjoy
the story!
Blessings,
Beth Ann
Baus

Beth Ann Baus

ISBN: 1720521859
ISBN-13: 978-1720521853

In loving memory of my father, Jimmy E. Franks; a messenger

ACKNOWLEDGMENTS

Thank you, Trinda Cole for your interest and encouragement during the early days of this project. Your edits and suggestions shaped Sister Sunday into what it is today. Chelsea Andres, I offer you my sincerest thanks and tightest of hugs. Thank you for reading, editing, re-reading and re-editing. But, thank you most of all for caring and sharing my excitement. Thank you, Brooke Gordon for your artistic eye behind the camera and Jasmine Petty for giving Delitha flesh and bone. Thank you, Alison from Sties Design Agency for putting all my pieces together and making something beautiful. I'm giving you each a standing ovation!

To all my friends and family who read my work and encouraged me to keep moving forward, thank you from the bottom of my heart. Your words were life giving and instrumental in this project coming to fruition.

My deepest gratitude goes to my husband, Chad, for encouraging me to follow this dream and for allowing me time to lose myself in a world that, for so long, existed only in my mind. Thank you for your help, your time, your patience and support. You are, and forever will be, my favorite person.

And, to my sons, Daniel and Levi, for giving life to my one dream greater than being an author. Being your mom is worth more to me than writing a thousand stories.

Sister Sunday

Desperate is the word my father used to describe our situation. Abandoned is the word he used to describe me. His letter dropped to the floor as I opened Aunt Esther's Bible to record Mother's death. It was then I realized my Aunt Esther had not come like an angel to save me. Instead, my father had given me away. I had not been rescued; I had been sent.

I traveled by train to attend Mother's burial. My head was pounding, my eyes sensitive to the light. Aunt Esther sat across from me with her hands folded neatly in her lap. Though her eyelids were pressed tightly together, I knew she was awake. She was thinking those inner most thoughts that can only be dealt with behind closed eyes. The eyes, they say, are a window to the soul and it is often necessary to keep those windows closed.

There are no words to describe what I felt as I saw the station nearing. There are no words to describe the sensation as I stepped off the train and breathed the fresh southern air into my lungs. It was as if I was moving in slow motion and everything around me had quickened its pace. It wasn't until Aunt Esther wrapped her arm around my waist that I realized my legs were beginning to give way. I don't remember much after that. I don't remember being reunited with my father. I don't remember dressing for Mother's service. I do, however, remember the feeling of relief. It spread over me like a warm blanket as I watched my father scatter a fistful of earth over Mother's coffin. That I remember well.

Had I only known then what I know now, I would have given her a proper goodbye. I would have woken her and held her before leaving her alone in her bed. I would have mourned and paid my respects before leaving her alone in the ground.

1

GEORGIA

1924

Mother had prayed for a litter of young girls to rear in her home. She had diligently asked the Lord to spare her from raising young boys. Mother was more familiar with the Word than any woman I knew, but raising young men to inherit my father's pulpit was a greater responsibility than she was willing to bear. "It is the wives," she would say, "that make the men who they ought to be." So, the challenge of raising "wives" was one she felt called to conquer. The Lord, I suppose, answered her prayers. He did not give her a son, nor did he give her a litter of girls. He simply gave her . . . me.

Mother shocked them all by surviving my arrival. She endured thirty-two hours of pain and bleeding, her mind fading in and out. There were prayers sent up on her behalf and there was talk of her never seeing the baby that tormented her from inside the womb. No one believed it was my fault, of course. I wasn't tormenting her on purpose. But, nonetheless, it was the life in my body that was taking the life from hers.

After what seemed like an eternity of suspense, Mother and I both opened our eyes to see, and our mouths to cry. Mother looked down at me with tears in her eyes, knowing this day would never come again, and she gave me all the names she had stored up for my sisters.

My name is Delitha. Delitha Susan Viney Missy Leigh. I alone represented the litter of girls that existed only in Mother's mind. Mother not only gave me five names, she gave me the responsibilities of the five bodies they should have belonged to. I honestly think when she looked at me she saw five figures; five little girls with five long ponytails and five sets of hands to help with the running of our home.

Mother called herself an innkeeper. I suppose in every sense of the term, she was just that. You see, Mother opened our front door to anyone who might be in need of a soft pillow on which to rest his or her head. Mother never met strangers and she never asked questions. She just loved them, every one of them. I can't begin to count the number of people that have passed through our house. People of all shapes and sizes, and as Mother put it, "people from all walks of life." Mother called herself an innkeeper. But, I know deep down Mother considered herself a saint. She kept a small journal under her mattress. I found it one time when she sent me upstairs to turn down the beds. I hadn't meant to pry; my hand seemed to flip through the pages with a mind of its own. I held my breath as I read. Scripted upon those pages were the names of every soul she had ever lent her hand to help. They were her points for getting inside the Great Kingdom.

As a child, I had no idea how many points it took to get inside the Great Kingdom. But I do remember bowing my head and praying that the Good Lord would let her know when she had enough. She would run up and down our stairs and stand over our stove till her entire body was red and wet with sweat. She would hand me a stack of plates, and I could hear her breathing in the next room as I set the tables. She worked hard. Hard enough, I thought, to earn points enough for the both of us.

My diddy was a gospel preacher. He was put on God's green earth to spread the truth, the light, and the way. I loved it when he said that. He would hold his Bible up over his head and tell me to kneel with him while he thanked God for His goodness. I suppose my diddy was trying to teach me how to pray, to be thankful. And, I suppose I did learn a thing or two about praying. Mostly, I learned to put a pillow down before I knelt. My diddy might keep me on my knees long enough to have made up every bed in our house. I learned to gently sway from side to side and put the pressure on one knee at a time. Sometimes I would sway anything but gently, and my diddy would place his hand on my back and say, "Lord, please give my daughter the patience to listen to our conversation, so that one day she might kneel here alone and converse with you herself."

My diddy loved me well. And, despite the five names my mother placed on me, he called me Del. It was my special name. It's the name I hear in my head when I picture my diddy's face. And how his face could light up a room! His teeth were bigger than any I had ever seen, and his eyelashes were so long, they rubbed up against the glasses that rested on his strong nose. I knew why people liked to listen to him. I'm certain it did have something to do with the good news he brought along, but I think it mostly had to do with how handsome he was. How his broad shoulders told those poor women he could carry their burdens. How his big hands told those children he could cradle them. And how his deep voice reminded the men of their own diddys. My diddy was a preacher, but he called himself a messenger.

It was the message that kept our town alive. The past six days of endless work and the thought of the next six quickly faded away as my diddy talked about the hope of a better life. Lives where we sit and eat for pleasure, not to satisfy a nagging hunger. A life where our only labor was the act of worship, which was not labor at all, but a willful desire. The message touched us all. And perhaps touched each of us in its own way. But for me, it wasn't the message as much as the gathering itself. After a long week in town at the inn, Sunday was the only day of the week I saw familiar faces. Faces belonging to good, hard-working people. Mostly farmers who were, good, God-fearing people. People such as Sister Murch with her crazy, larger-than-life hats that were fascinating to look at yet impossible to sit behind. There were Brother Earsel and Sister Erma Long with their matching hand-carved walking sticks. There was the Wood family, whose children teased me for my pointy eyeteeth when all eight of their noses crooked to the left as if something to the right of them had a foul smell. But, there was one family I ached for when we were apart. Mr. and Mrs. Sunday, along with their five children, whose clay-colored freckles covered every inch of their bodies. It was their family that brought my rest.

John and Carolyn Sunday were the best of friends with Mother and my diddy. Before we moved to town, our families would gather together every Saturday night. My diddy said it was his way of clearing his mind before presenting his message the next morning. Mother and Carolyn would quilt and gossip while my diddy and Mr. Sunday sat on the porch with their pipes, discussing the crops and how the yields would be low if the rain didn't come or go very soon.

There was Jack, Luke, Simon, and Albert who sat in the corner whittling doll furniture for their little sister, Ida. The boys adored and protected her as if they were all four her legal guardians. Even Albert, who was only two years her senior. But, no matter how much they cared for Ida, their love for her was no match to my own. I loved everything about her. From her red hair and freckled face, to her large feet that seemed to point inward as she walked. Her voice was high pitched and her laugh was awkward, but it was all music to my ears. Ida represented the steadfastness that I lacked. She was my anchor. My constant.

Ida and I couldn't have been much over three years old when we started pretending we were sisters. For Ida, it was simply for companionship. Why wouldn't she wish to have a sister among all those boys? But for me, it was more than that. For me, it was wishing for a new family. A different family. Specifically, a different mother.

I often wondered if Mother knew just how much I hated her. If she even realized the pain she caused me. Perhaps she knew. Or, perhaps she was simply oblivious to how her life was affecting mine. It doesn't really matter, you know. Her motive is of no importance. Those years are long gone. Buried along with her. All that is left are the memories; the sore spots that only I know how to dance around. It never ceases to amaze me, though, how the slightest thing can take me back there. How a taste or scent can send me back to that kitchen with Mother swatting my hand with her wooden spoon. A simple swipe of fabric can put me back in the guest bedrooms making and remaking the beds until she was pleased. Mother comes back to me when I brush my hair in the evening. She would yank at the tangles with her fingers rather than with my brush, pulling and tugging with all her might; I knew better than to scream or cry aloud. I would sit gripping my dress until my knuckles were white; and although my lips were tightly pressed together, I could taste my tears and the runs from my nose.

Our guests, whom I often heard snoring in the next room, never knew of my pain. I kept my tears, best I could, for my pillow. My pillowcase, which has long since been discarded, was stained with my silent weeping. With the covers pulled high over my head and my face buried, I would expel every emotion that had built up throughout the day. My bed, that tiny feather mattress on an iron frame that squeaked at the slightest movement, was my only release. Looking back, it was less about the bed and more about the dark that brought me comfort. There was security in the blackness that surrounded me. I couldn't see anything; therefore, nothing could see me. I was alone.

There were days when I would find myself crawling under those heavy blankets for a quick moment of solitude. Days when Mother's temper equaled the temperatures outside our house. One day in particular, I remember having cleared the tables after lunch and was drawing water to wash the dishes. Mother entered the kitchen just as I was tightening the apron that hung around my waist. "Move," was all she said to me. Her face was red and her breathing was heavy. Her hands were shaking as she reached for my shoulders, shoving me to the side. "Move," she said again. I fell against the small breakfast table that sat in the middle of our kitchen. Its corner met my rib cage, stealing my breath for a moment. As I turned, trying to stand straight, I found Mother hunched over digging into a basket under the sink. After a moment she let out a sigh and stuffed something under her apron. Spinning around she stood and grabbed my arm. "Go to your room," she hissed.

"But, the dishes . . ."

"Forget the dishes; I'll do the dishes. Just get out my sight for a few minutes."

She escorted me to the bottom of the stairs, pointed to my bedroom door, and darted back into the kitchen. A moment later I stood in the center of my room, my own face red, my own breathing heavy. The windows in my room were raised, as were all the windows that time of year. The shears hung heavy as there was no breeze to help them sway. The air was dead, heavy, and hot. I remember standing there staring at the open window, watching the heat pour in over the sills. "If this house were a boat, I would be drowning." I said aloud. "Perhaps I will suffocate instead."

With that thought, I crawled into my bed and pulled the covers high over my head. My skin was prickly and wet with sweat. My heart was racing and seemed to randomly skip a beat. My stomach threatened to reproduce what I had taken in that morning and my lungs burned every time the word 'suffocate' passed through my mind. Yet, there was a faint smile on my face. There was relief in my aching muscles. I was alone. And, if by chance I did succeed in suffocating myself under those sweaty sheets, I knew whatever awaited me on the other side, had to be better than where I was.

2

Looking back, I suppose I should have seen the signs. I have countless memories of Mother digging through a secret hiding space, tucking something under her apron, and sending me out of the room. How could I not have known? I remember thinking that she had found a special something that had been misplaced, and upon finding it, she would realize that I wasn't special enough to share the treasure with, and therefore send me out of the room. Sounds silly doesn't it? It's amazing the guilt children put on themselves to preserve the likes of their parents.

There was a short period however, when Mother seemed better. My diddy had been traveling regularly to the city to visit his father who had become very ill. Grandfather was not expected to live long and my diddy, as the only son, did his duty by staying close to his side during his final days. I dare not say she was better while my diddy was gone; rather, she was different. She seemed to sleep longer when my diddy was gone. I would find myself serving breakfast to our guests as she was just making her way downstairs. And although I would have expected her to fly about the house in a mad rush, trying desperately to make up for lost time, she would come and sit in the kitchen and chat with me while I worked. She would often act as though she too were a guest.

The betterment came after diddy's telegram arrived, announcing Grandfather's death. She called on Ms. Mary and Ms. Charity Longing to run the inn while we were away. Mary and Charity were two sisters, both too old to be unwed and living together, or so my mother would say about them. However, they were hard-working and trustworthy, not to mention overjoyed when mother referred to the amount she would pay them for their services. I remember my own jaw dropping as I heard her generous offer. Mother was more than frugal; she was cheap. Not that we had extra money lying around, but Mother lived as though we had no money at all.

It wasn't until our arrival at Grandfather's house that her actions made sense to me. His home, or as Mother called it, his estate, was the largest in town until his neighbor built his own monstrosity next door in an effort to prove himself. Grandfather's landscaping was just as immaculate as the furnishings inside. And as folks passed by, they would either raise their heads in awe or bow their heads with a pang of unworthiness. I, myself, had spent very little time at Grandfather's estate. He had come to the country a handful of times to visit us, but our visits to town were few and far between. My memories of that place were as old and dusty as the family photograph that set upon my diddy's desk.

What grabbed my attention as we walked in the door was the expression on Mother's face. She hurried from room to room as if she were sweeping the floors with the hem of her skirt. Her hands brushed over all the tables and chairs that seemed to be strategically placed in each room. Mother had covered the entire first floor before I had passed over the foyer. I remember standing, looking down at my feet. Or rather at the rug I stood on. The state of the home was not as I expected. Grandfather had been sick for some time, and I imagined every corner being filled with cobwebs and the floors covered in balls of dust. I had even covered my mouth as I entered expecting the stench of death. But, to my surprise, Grandfather's home was very much alive. The air was sweet and the floors and corners clean; there were live ferns scattered around each room and vases of bright red roses set in the center of each table.

There was music coming from the back parlor and its melody seemed to beckon my inner soul. My body moved toward the sound without the permission of my feet, and as I turned the corner my eyes set upon a sight I had never seen before. A large gramophone sat in the corner of the room, sparkling as if it had been freshly polished. Even the music spilling from its gut seemed to sparkle in the air. Kneeling in front of the gramophone was a twisted figure I couldn't recognize at first glance. The body was shaking; sobbing. It wasn't until she looked up, startled by my presence, that I realized it was Mother. Her face was dripping with tears; her eyes seemed as soft and kind as any I'd ever seen.

"Praise God!" she said, rushing at me on her knees. Mother wrapped her arms around my waist and hugged me as though there were true love between us.

"This," she whispered, looking up at me, "It's all ours. All of it! Everything!" She reached up and grasped my shoulders forcing me to look her straight in the eye. The force behind her whisper caused strands of my hair to fly back from my face. "Isn't it wonderful, Delitha? Our day has finally come."

Before I could answer, my diddy appeared at the room's entrance.

"Beverly, you've arrived." His voice was soft, tired. I detected a hint of relief.

"Oh, Walter," Mother gathered herself and leapt into his arms. "I am so terribly sorry, my Darling. I do hope your grief has not overcome you."

He didn't respond, at least not with words. They stood and held one another, lost in the moment.

By nightfall, we had all found our place of comfort. I sat on the back porch, amazed that the stars looked the same in town as they did at home in the country. My diddy had spent hours in Grandfather's study, flipping through old books and papers. He retired in the kitchen, no doubt meditating on what he had lost. Mother had spent a half hour or so sitting in each room of the house, surveying them from different angles, examining different pieces of furniture and staring hard at different portraits that hung on the walls. Mother was no doubt meditating on all she had gained.

Grandfather was buried on a Tuesday. I was eight years old. We were all dressed in black and I will never forget how grown up I felt. I will also never forget Mother standing under that great oak shaking her head.

"What's the matter, Mother?" I asked her, wiping tears and rain from my face.

"This isn't what I expected," she said solemnly. "I always thought your Grandfather held the Lord's favor."

"I don't understand," I confessed.

"The weather, child. The rain reveals a great deal of your Grandfather's standing with his Maker. I had expected sunshine on the day we gave him back to the earth, back to his Maker's hands."

Mother had her faults, but one thing I never questioned was her understanding of the Lord. She spoke of Him with such confidence; it never occurred to me that she might be wrong. Although I had never heard of the Lord confirming His likes or dislikes of any man by the weather, if Mother said it, it must be so.

While Mother stood, still shaking her head, I moved toward my diddy, who was holding the arm of another woman. Her high heels set her an inch above my diddy and her hat added another inch above that. Her hands were hidden under satin gloves and my diddy held a swan-necked umbrella over them as they stood whispering at one another. The brim of her hat covered her face, only her lips were exposed. They seemed to be sharing secrets with one another. The closer I got to them, the more my eyes focused in on her mouth. Her lips were perfectly rounded, and there was a brown mole on the side of her chin that seemed to shrink or grow depending on how her mouth moved.

They looked so natural together, more so than he and Mother. I was on her heels ready to make my arrival known when Mother dashed up behind me and steered me in the opposite direction.

"We don't want to bother your father, right now."

"Who is that woman? I wanted to meet her."

"She's no one you need to know."

"But . . ."

"Leave it alone, Delitha. She's no one!"

Mother escorted me back to our carriage. She lifted me rather than allowing me to climb in. A small piece of hair let loose from its pin and wrapped itself around her jaw. Mother quickly jerked her head sending the lock out of her way, though it disobediently slid down her cheek again.

"Sit here," she said to me, "we'll be leaving soon."

As she pushed me in, my muddy feet wiped themselves on the hem of my dress. As I slid from Mother's grip and into my seat, my cheek brushed against hers. The lost strand of hair felt like silk against my face, and I couldn't remember ever being that close to her, so close that she was out of focus. In the moment it took our faces to pass by one another, I remember hearing a voice in my head, "She's so pretty." Her skin was soft and flawless. Her cheeks were flushed and her breath smelled sweet. She was almost beautiful. Mother took a few steps, and then turned back to me. She did not speak audibly, but her lips were never hard to read. "Stay put!" she said, overemphasizing the word "stay." As her face twisted, the beauty that had revealed itself to me quickly fled from my mind.

Mother moved quickly toward my diddy, waving her arms to get his attention. Before Mother arrived at his side, he had embraced and moved away from this mystery woman, the woman with the secrets. I watched as this seemingly harmless creature took long strides, never looking back, walking with confidence as though someone were waiting for her. But, there was no one. My eyes followed her across the lawn, up a small embankment, and to a small black carriage where a man in a round hat nodded and took her arm, helping her to step in. She folded herself into the seat, the round hatted man took his seat before her, and they were off. I sat and watched her disappear down the lane. Whoever she was, she was gone. My mind raced with questions as my parents took their seats on either side of me for the long, silent ride home.

We were settled into Grandfather's estate within the month. I don't remember feeling much of anything as we left our home in the country. It had been a good home, the walls were sturdy and the roof kept the rain out. There was a draft at my window and the floor let out a creak under my feet when I stepped out of bed, but it was a good home. It was sure to be more than enough for the next family. My silent prayer for this family was that they would fill the house with pleasant memories. Those walls held in many secrets, many burdens, many nightmares come to life. My prayer was for a new family to open the windows and drain that house empty, start from scratch, and then fill it with love.

Love, I have been told, is as natural as the tide, especially between a child and its mother. It was Mrs. Sunday that said this to me, after sharing a sweet moment of endearment with Ida. "I have never seen the tide," I told her. I had never felt the rejuvenating power she spoke of so freely. It was on that night, tucked beneath a stack of hand-stitched quilts, that Ida asked me to close my eyes, think of Mother, and describe the first image that came to mind. I found myself on the riverbank. I couldn't have been more than three or four years old. My diddy had taken us fishing for the afternoon after church, and Mother had snagged her forefinger with her hook. She never made a sound. She simply examined the wound and slid her finger in her mouth. This was something I had seen my diddy do many times, but what struck me was the look on her face. The look of satisfaction, as if she enjoyed the taste of blood in her mouth. She held it there, suckling it as if she were a child holding fast to her milk bottle. The look on her face scared me, something in me knew that wouldn't be the last time I would see her eyes glazed over as she savored the flavor on her tongue.

I was right, you know. That day on the riverbank was only the beginning. It was only a few days after that, Mother slit her finger while slicing a loaf of bread. Her eyes glazed over the instant she shoved the broken skin in her mouth. It became almost predictable. If I didn't know better, I would think she had cut herself on purpose. After a few months, even my diddy stopped inquiring about her new cuts. We accepted them, just as we accept the sun rising and falling with the day.

Acceptance . . . now this was something I learned early on. I accepted the parents I was given. I accepted the disappointment I had brought to Mother. I accepted the daily struggles of her tough love. I accepted the move from everything I knew and held dear. I accepted the fact that the only change was the walls that held us together, the floors that led us from one confrontation to the next, and the roof that held the word family over our heads. It seemed as though my life would never change, and that too was something I accepted, just as I accepted the notion that the brilliance of the tide was not meant for me.

3

Grandfather's home was much larger than what we had known in the country, and Mother seemed almost giddy at the thought of how many more people we could accommodate. I, on the other hand, was exasperated by the mere thought of it. We had occupied the home for no more than a month when Mother posted the vacancy sign on the front porch and a sign in the yard that read, "Come to me, ye who are weary and heavy laden, and I will give you rest."

Two days later, just after sunrise, there came a knock at the door. A small man with curly white hair stood before me. He carried with him one camel-colored bag that was bulging at the seams and a handful of letters tightly bound by a yellow ribbon. His skin was brown, not from the sun or from his heritage, but from dirt.

"My name's Sim," he said with a scratchy voice. "I'm lookin' for a place to rest for a day or two. Won't be much bother to ya'll. Don't eat much, not much by way of conversation neither. Just need a place to rest."

He slumped before me with a tired back and a broken spirit. I hadn't known what to say to him, or to anyone for that matter. I had never been allowed to speak with our guests. Only to serve them. I stood there with my mouth clamped tight until I heard Mother's footsteps coming up behind me. I turned to her, then back to the small man. "This is Sim," I told her. "He isn't hungry, just tired."

Mother stepped on my foot as she pushed her way ahead of me. "Hungry or not, every guest gets a hot meal." She smiled and gestured inside the house. "Do come in, sir."

Sim was true to his word. He hardly touched the stew I had prepared or the coffee I had brewed. He spoke only when spoken to and disappeared into his room for over thirty-six hours. To date, he was the most pleasant guest I have tended to. With every guest that passed through this house, Mother's kindness seemed to increase tenfold, her openness seemed to extend to everyone, everyone that is, but me.

It seemed as though Mother had only energy enough for strangers. The more strangers she tended to, the less she tended to those who knew her best. But, looking back, I wonder if anyone really knew her. Even my diddy seemed to look at her with the same eyes as he did his flock. Lovingly, but with distant eyes.

We were now a good hour's ride to our church. My diddy designated one day a week to spend in the country and make his rounds. Although his intentions were to help with the running of the inn, he spent his other days forming relationships with the other folk in town. That left me to bear Mother alone. Her mood swings, that were once as predictable as a pendulum on a clock, were now swinging at me like an owl swooping from the shadows to attack its prey.

The people in town were extremely kind. Ladies would stop in to meet Mother and see what changes the home had undergone. They all left, however, disappointed. Mother had not moved one single item in the entire house. Above her bed she had framed and hung their marriage license. Above my bed was a document declaring my birth and baptism. We had pounded two nails in the kitchen wall on which to hang our aprons. Extra tables were added in the dining hall for our guests. Other than these simple additions, the home was just as Grandfather had left it.

My responsibilities seemed to multiply with each passing day. Although Mother took to the cooking, I was given the duty of serving, refilling, clearing, cleaning, and resetting the room for the next meal. Although Mother enjoyed hanging the laundry and watching it flap in the wind, I was given the duty of undressing, washing, and redressing the beds, as well as keeping towels and clean water in each room and washing out the basins each morning. Mother enjoyed sweeping off the front and back porch when the day's work was done. I was then allowed, after our guests had turned in for the night, to do whatever might be pleasing to me.

I found my solace under a giant weeping willow at the north corner of our land. Ol' Willy, as I named the tree, became my reward after a long day of work. I sat beneath his large branches to read books, to write letters, or to simply sit and be alone, to enjoy the silence. There were two branches that formed a small separation, just enough to expose the moonlight and the twinkling of the stars.

Ida was allowed to stay with us once a month or so. Mother would send home bread and cobblers in exchange for her help with our guests. We would rush around all day finishing our chores, longing for the seclusion we knew awaited us under that tree. Beneath those lanky branches, we would play house or make hair ribbons out of grass and dandelions. Ida would sing songs, and I would sketch her profile as she posed against the large, coarse trunk. It was our world, our time. It was our source of joy, the source of our hearts staying young while our hands and feet callused from the day's work.

As the years passed, our talk of dolls changed to talk of boys. We would slip apples in our dresses and dream of being women. Ida even used Ol' Willy to practice kissing. "Should I ever find myself in the arms of one of the Lansing brothers," she would whisper, "it would be in my best interest to know what on earth I'm doing!"

As often as we talked and laughed about boys and how we might go about getting their attention, I always knew that Ida was serious and that I was not. There was something in me that longed for someone older, wiser than the boys that pulled our hair and teased us at church. They say that men marry their mothers, that they find themselves most attracted to that which raised them. I often wondered if that were true for me. Perhaps I was searching for someone holding the qualities I loved so much in my diddy. The notion hardly seemed unreasonable to me, yet I never shared that with Ida. That, undoubtedly, was the only childhood secret I ever kept from her.

"Secrets," Mother would growl, "are from the devil." This was the gospel Mother preached to herself to step around her addiction to gossip. Ida's mother, Carolyn, knew better than to question Mother's knowledge on what was and wasn't from the devil. Therefore, out of fear for her own precious salvation, she offered up any and all goods she had on any and all she knew. Mother, on the other hand, was quick to rebuke gossip, seeing how it too was from the devil. So, after an hour or so of soaking in all the new gossip, she would solemnly swear to keep any and all information a secret.

Ida, on the other hand, believed in one thing, that God gave us ears to hear and mouths to repeat it. And what better place to share the secrets of God's children, than in our Father's Holy House.

"Where's Jack?" I asked taking my seat next to the Sunday family.

"He went and got married," she answered with wide eyes.

21

"Married?"

"Last night, he and Laura McDow went to . . . well, they went to your house. Your daddy married them."

My mind went blank for a moment. Where had I been? Was I sleeping? Why did no one wake me? Why wasn't I told over breakfast? Could that explain why Mother had not responded to my diddy when he offered her good morning?

"Mama wouldn't let us go," she whispered. "Mama said they should just get it over with and move on now that Laura's . . ." Before she could finish, Albert gave her an elbow in the ribs. "We ain't supposed to talk about it, now shush."

Ida and I looked at him, then at each other. Ida patted her belly and her eyes grew even wider.

The fact that Jack had married and "moved on" had no direct impact on me other than my seat. We had moved down to fill his spot on the pew and now I was seated directly in front of old Sister Vander. She was a rather large woman who sat with great discomfort. She also sat with one hand gripping the seat in front of her, placing her knuckles directly under my left shoulder. It was then that I realized why Ida had sat up straight in her seat, sitting at the edge as if she were eagerly awaiting the chance to stand. "This too shall pass," I told myself as I sat forward and glared at the cross pendant dangling from my diddy's Bible.

And, it did pass. Two months later we were singing hymns as Luke and Virginia Mae exchanged vows under the blue summer sky. Virginia wore baby's breath in her hair and "they kissed for an unacceptable amount of time," Mother noted. That day, Ida watched with pure envy as her brother introduced Virginia as his wife. But, my thoughts rested solely on the fact that, come Sunday morning, I could scoot down one more spot and rest my back flat against the wooden bench.

"Suppose I become an old spinster?" Ida asked. She directed the question to the sky rather than to me. We were walking into the trees now, away from the celebration, away from Virginia Mae. I gave Ida a slight nudge with my shoulder. "At what age is a woman considered an old spinster?"

"I'm not certain, only I know it's far before she should actually be referred to as 'old'."

"Ida," I reminded her, "you're only twelve years old. Now, that's enough talk. Shall we swim or pick berries?" The sun was beating down on me and I prayed she would answer swim.

Her actions spoke for her. Running toward the pond, she only glanced back at me for a moment, long enough to show me her devilish grin.

"Ida Sunday, if you don't take off that dress . . ." Before she could heed my warning, Ida had jumped feet first into the pond. Seconds later, she came up gasping for air and pushing the hair and ribbons from her eyes. She was so lovely. There was no doubt she would capture the heart of a man. Whenever it happened though, it wouldn't be soon enough for her liking.

"Ida, your mama made that dress special for today! She'll tan your hide!"

"My mama made your dress special for today too!" she sputtered, still trying to catch her breath.

"I don't much like this dress," I confessed under those blasting rays of sun, and with that I found myself floating next to my best friend in the whole world, drenched and defiant.

Defiance was not typically in my nature. Nor was it in Ida's for that matter. But every now and then it seemed as though there were some unbeatable force inside us driving us to wrongdoing. On that day, I could have blamed it on the heat. Heat, so I've been told, can make people think and act in ways they would never dream of in a normal situation. Ida's father had suffered a heat stroke three summer's prior and Ida says he was uttering words she wouldn't dare repeat. Yes, the heat would have been a valid excuse. Or our youth, I could have argued, played some small role in it. Perhaps it was our cry for independence. Whatever the reason, that day we chose to jump in that pond fully dressed the same way we chose to hide poison ivy in Virginia Mae's bouquet.

"Look at me!" Ida screamed, drawing my attention back to her. She had swum to the center of the pond and was climbing aboard a floating dock.

"How do I look? And if you're not going to say stunning then you'd best keep your mouth shut."

Ida was quite the actress. Her expressions were so animated I often found myself watching her eyes and following her hand motions and then realizing I had given no attention to the actual story she was telling. She was like a one-man band; only in her case, she was a one-woman play.

"You look absolutely stunning," I said, making my way to the dock. It was quite a chore, mind you, to swim fully clothed.

"Do you think I stand a chance at becoming the next Peach Queen?"

"Why on earth would you want to be the Peach Queen?" I asked. "For the rest of your life all people will think of when they see you are peaches."

Ida pushed her eyebrows together.

"There she is, they'll say, the girl who had her picture taken with a giant peach."

"Well," Ida snapped. "What's better than being remembered for your favorite food?"

"Since when are peaches your favorite food?"

"Peaches have always been my favorite food," she said as sincerely as she could. "Ever since I was a baby. Because they are sweet and juicy and furry and . . . well, they're peachy!" she exclaimed.

"You almost convinced me," I told her. "Can you convince the judges?"

Ida picked up her dress and bunched it up around her waist; water trickled down her legs as she kicked up her heels.

"I could woo the judges, just give me the chance," she cried out as she leaped around the dock.

Together we began stepping along all four sides of the dock as if we were on a tightrope. Dresses picked up, legs reaching out as far as they could go, toes pointed like those belonging to a ballerina. We walked slowly at first getting used to the dock moving with us, and then we began to pick up our pace. I continued around the edges of the dock as Ida began twisting and twirling in the middle. Tiny water droplets sprung from our bodies and glistened around us like flakes of glitter.

"If they could see me dance," she giggled, "they'd have to crown me Queen!"

"Well, Ida, I have to say, after today I don't think your mother will agree to make your dress."

"Oh, who needs a new dress anyway? In fact, let's just change the rules. Let's base this competition on who looks best in their underpants!" By now, Ida was laughing so hard she could hardly keep her balance, and we grabbed on to one another to keep from going overboard.

"Tell me the truth, Judge Number One . . . what do you think?"

She winked at me and began unzipping her dress. She wiggled and jumped in place to reach behind her back.

"I don't think you'll win on your gracefulness," I snickered, as I sat down at her feet to steady the dock.

By the time I caught the breath my laughter had stolen, Ida had completely removed her new dress and was swinging it over her head. As drenched as it was, neither of us were surprised when it slipped right out of her hand and back into the water. Our laughter was uncontrollable and our echo seemed to bounce off the surrounding trees and rush back over our faces.

"Perhaps we could add a talent contest as well," she said, her face hidden by her enormous smile.

"What on earth is your talent? You can hardly walk a straight line!" I tugged at her legs almost bringing her down. She bent over gripping my shoulders to steady herself.

"I would sing." She stood again with a renewed confidence. And to this day, I'm not certain what it was she was trying to sing. But, she sang through her laughter until tears began spilling down her cheeks and landed at my feet.

"It should have been me," she whispered. "It should have been me."

"Your day will come," I said, standing to join her. "Besides, if that had been you, then you'd be married to your brother right now."

She smiled then quickly wiped it away.

"Don't be in such a hurry to grow up, Ida. Once these days are gone, you'll never get them back." I said this exactly the way my diddy had said it to me, only weeks before.

"Would that be so bad?" she asked.

I stiffened and had no answer. Just questions. Why, for instance, did Ida want to grow up so quickly? Her life was perfect. Why would she want out of it? It was that day I realized that no matter how good or bad your life is, we all want out. Simply because we want to make our life our own.

"Where do you want to go?" she asked, rubbing her cheeks with the backs of her hands.

"What?"

"I want to go to Atlanta and be crowned the Peach Queen. I want to be beautiful! What do you want?"

I hesitated. What did I want? That was a question I had asked myself a thousand times but never had anyone else thought to ask.

"I want to go somewhere safe, where I can figure out who I'm supposed to be."

Ida wrapped her arms around me and whispered, "One day you'll find that place. And one day someone will tell me how beautiful I am."

There we stood, drenched, embracing, with Ida only half-dressed.

"Peach Queen or not, I think you're perfect, Ida. Your day will come."

"You're my best friend," we whispered simultaneously. Then, without hesitation, Ida kissed me on the cheek. She lingered there for a moment and her lips felt cool on my warm skin. Her hair smelled of fresh honeysuckle. This kiss, this gesture, was one we had shared only a few times in our friendship. One that reminded us both of the love we shared. A love most commonly found between sisters. A love we had felt for no other. We stood there feeling the drippings collect under our feet, then as unexpected as it had come, the silence was broken.

"Delitha! You come here this instant!" Mother's voice raced across the water and forced itself on us. I looked at her, followed the voice to its source. Ida's mother stood a few steps behind. She stood with her hands clasped together. Her head was down.

"I said this instant. Move!"

Despite the intensity in her voice, our release was slow and steady.

"I'll see you next Sunday then." There were still tears in her eyes.

"If my head is still sitting in its place, I'll see you next Sunday." I returned her kiss quickly, almost knocking her off-balance. "Now, dry those eyes. We deduct points from contestants who can't control their emotions." She smiled, and for a brief moment I forgot about the curse that awaited me on the shore.

The water hit my face smooth, like the wind. I swam the distance with little effort. I kept myself under the water as long as possible, hoping that when I emerged, Mother would have returned to the party. However, I have never been one with any luck to brag about. Coming out of the water, my body felt heavier than I had anticipated and I stumbled on the loose rocks. My bare hands broke my fall, the rocks scraping the skin from both palms. I caught my balance, stood, and lifted my hands watching as the water mixed with my blood, giving the appearance of being more than there really was. As the blood began slipping down to my wrists, I looked up meeting Mother's eyes. They were oversized and bloodshot. Before I moved another muscle, her open hand swept across my face, sending my head bobbing to the side.

This was not the first or last time I would feel her hand sweep across my face. It was, however, the first time I uttered those dreadful words. The words no parent wants to hear. I told her I hated her. My expectations of her reaction were not only met, but exceeded. Mother stumbled over to a great maple and sat beneath its shade. This was only the second time I had seen her cry.

Ida fished her dress from the water and after forcing her body back inside it, she and her mother walked back to the picnic hand in hand. Her mother whispered and shook her head as they walked. I was eaten up with envy as I watched them walk away. Ida and her mother, their fingers intertwined like the roots of a tree. Their love was strong. Their roots could not be untangled.

4

Mother greeted me the next morning with a renewed spirit. She was almost giddy. She was laughing and sharing jokes with our guests in a way that made me question the day before. Had she really been so angry as to raise her hand to me? I felt a strange discomfort as she patted my back when I entered the kitchen.

"Good morning, sleepyhead."

"Good morning, Mother." Her voice was higher than normal and mine seemed a notch lower.

"There is a plate for you on the table, under the towel. Eat up before it gets cold, then I'll need your help clearing the dining room." She opened the door with her back, holding a full cup of tea in each hand. I could hear her making the delivery, "How is everything? Can I get you more gravy? More jam?" To her surprise I was still standing in the same spot when she returned. "Delitha, dear. Is everything all right? Are you ill?" she placed her hand on my forehead long enough to check for fever, then she picked up a tray of condiments and made her way out the door again, whispering as she exited, "Eat up."

On my plate I found a biscuit smothered in gravy, a slice of ham, and a small pile of scrambled eggs. This was the typical breakfast we served to our guests but never to ourselves. I usually feasted on a bowl of room-temperature oatmeal, long after the guests had been served, the tables cleared, and the dishes washed and put away. I was certain this was a dream, although my taste buds told me otherwise. The fresh-squeezed orange juice was ice-cold, and I could feel it make its way down my throat and into my stomach. I could have traced its course with my finger. The biscuits were buttermilk, Mother's specialty, the kind she made back home in the country. Not realizing how much I'd missed them, my mouth began watering before I even took the first bite. I literally closed my eyes before swallowing, trying to savor the moment, the flavor, of home.

Only, this home existed in my head, in my heart. A home I dreamed of, being envious of others who possessed it. I held on to the moment, knowing it was only a matter of time before the sweetness would turn sour. It was only a matter of time before Mother's other self would come to life. She would force my other self to come to life as well . . . the self that becomes invisible, complacent, and apologetic. It's the side of me that is numb to insults. Numb to life. It is the side of me that defies all we know to be true, the side of me that walks the earth although it is dead.

My prediction was correct. Her sweetness lasted only until the following morning. "There are eight beds that need to be made within the hour." She growled.

"Yes, ma'am."

"You look as though a dog drug you in during the night. Go to your room this instant and wash your face. If you can't tame that head of hair then put on a covering."

"Yes, ma'am."

My breakfast dishes had been washed and put away. The table wiped down. I moved from the cupboard toward the door when Mother grabbed my arm. Her grip was tight enough to make my hand feel fat. A fist formed, and without thinking I began opening and closing it.

"You've got the speed of a snail." She pulled me through the door to the landing before the staircase. Releasing my arm, she stood silent, simply pointing up the stairs. I skipped the first step and sprinted upward.

"Delitha! A lady does not run! Steady your pace or I will have you in the linen closet for the remainder of the day!"

I ignored her threat, as I always did. She was quick to raise her hand to me, but condemning me to the linen closet meant condemning herself to finishing the chores.

We set off, walking, in different directions. I heard one of our guests greet her, complimenting the meal. "Oh, you are so kind," she responded, in her sweetest voice. "If there is anything, anything at all I can do to make your stay more comfortable, please don't hesitate to ask."

"I am quite comfortable. Thank you."

I watched as he tipped his hat to her before heading for the door. He wore brown trousers, held up by suspenders. The sleeves of his white shirt were folded to his forearm. He turned the doorknob but did not open the door. Instead, he turned and raised his attention to the balcony. Mr. Peck stayed with us once a month while in town for business. He owned a small lumber company in Swansboro but did his banking here in Savannah. Tipping his hat to me, as he had to Mother, he placed his other hand on the arm of our hall tree, leaving a small piece of hard candy. "Good day," he said with a smile.

My brain knew what to do in this situation. Mr. Peck had tempted my taste buds this way before. My brain told me to walk away, to let someone else find the candy. That, however, posed another problem. What if no one else found it? What if it were knocked onto the floor and swept up into the garbage. The thought of wasting that piece of candy was more than I could bear. I remember leaning over the balcony to make certain Mother had made her way out of sight, which she had. Closing my eyes for a brief second, I sucked in my breath and took off down the stairs. My feet hit the bottom step with a louder than expected thump and I seemed to slide across the foyer with my hand landing directly over the piece of candy. "Contact," I whispered to myself as I raised my hand and slid the slender cherry-flavored treat in my mouth. A smile actually formed on my face as the first bit of sugar ran down my throat.

As I turned to sprint back up the stairs, I caught a shadow out of the corner of my eye. This time her target was not my face, or my bottom, rather the middle of my back. Her hand landed so hard and so flat against my spine, it sent the entire piece of candy sailing down my throat, causing an instant burn in my chest.

"I don't mean to raise a child that can't follow simple directions." Again she led me to the stairs; only this time, she led me all the way to my door.

"Psalm 79:9," she whispered pulling me into her.

"Help us," I whispered back to her. "O God our Savior, for the glory of Your name; deliver us and forgive our sins for Your name's sake."

Quoting the Word was a daily practice in our house, although it was associated with punishment, not pleasure. When I was very young, Mother rewarded me for putting verses to memory. But, when I turned ten years of age she decided I was old enough to remember on my own. She sat me down one day and said, "Instead of rewarding you with sweets, I'm going to remember you in my prayers." I knew even then what an honor it was to be added to Mother's prayer list. She believed that the Lord commanded us to pray but did not command us to ramble. Therefore, Mother strictly dedicated one half-hour per day to talking with the Lord. I knew she spent a good part of that time praying for all the travelers staying in our home. So, the number of guests we had determined who else got mentioned.

Not so much now, but then, I thought Mother's prayers were more holy than those of my diddy. My diddy prayed because he was a preacher and because he needed someone to talk to. Mother prayed because she feared what might happen if she did not. I figured the Lord would rather listen to a woman in fear than a man who makes his daughter kneel to listen to his one-sided conversations. I was probably wrong. I don't claim to know the ways of our Lord. But, I do claim to know this. I know that in my twelfth year, our household began to change. Perhaps I should have seen it coming, but after all, I was only a child.

5

It was a beautiful Sunday morning. The sky was clear, the birds were singing, the smell of bacon swept under my door. I woke with no particular change to my appearance, or to my overall being. Yet I was, on that day, turning an entire year older. It was my twelfth birthday. The sun shown perfectly into my room, giving me more than adequate light to prepare myself for the day ahead. The bare wood beneath my feet seemed warm and the cotton dress I slipped on seemed extraordinarily soft. I hopped down the stairs to the kitchen, paying extra attention to the men exchanging pleasantries in the foyer. I passed by them as though I were invisible.

Our family had few traditions. But one tradition we could always count on was the birthday breakfast. No matter the day or the weather, the one with the birthday chose whatever and however much they wanted for breakfast that day. This process was always a surprise with my diddy. He always chose something new and exciting. He might choose pancakes with the most unlikely of side dishes, or a pastry filled with ingredients we had never thought to put together. I looked forward to diddy's birthday breakfast as much as he did. Mother, on the other hand, would choose a boring combination of tea and crackers or coffee with a plain biscuit. She seemed to find pleasure in disappointing our desires to treat her. I suppose my request was no surprise either, but it was indeed a treat. Hot apple dumplings with a scoop of vanilla ice cream. No one bothered to ask me anymore; I had given the same answer since we started the tradition, on my fourth birthday.

That morning as I entered the kitchen, my eyes went from the bare table to my diddy standing over the sink taking in the last of his morning coffee. He turned his tired eyes to me as I stepped toward him.

"Good morning, Del." He placed his cup in the sink and slowly embraced me. He held me at arm's length and studied me a moment before speaking.

"Listen. Your mother isn't feeling well this morning. I need you to stay here with her. I won't stay for the picnic, I'll head home immediately following the services."

"Yes, sir" was all I could muster out of my disappointment. I held my tears back until he had left the room.

There would be little to do while my diddy was gone. On Sundays, our guests received a small breakfast, and a small snack before bed. The beds were not changed, the floors were not swept. Only the water in the basins was refreshed. And assuming Mother had not done so, I moved to each room and refilled the water pitchers. I could hear Mother moaning from behind her closed door. Every once in a while I would hear her bed springs wrenching beneath her. I had made up my mind first thing that I would only check on her if I heard her calling for me. Then I decided that even if she called for me, I was afraid to go to her aid.

I retreated to Ol' Willy, angry that Mother had ruined my day. The 'my day' I had been waiting an entire year for.

"She's sick," I told him. "She's been in bed all morning and I had to stay home to look after her. Now I have to wait another seven days to see Ida." I snuggled up to his trunk and ran my finger in and out of the grooves in his bark. "What if something important happened this week? If she forgets by next week, I'll never know." A branch blew and ruffled my hair. I stretched out and placed my face on the cool earth. I rested there not knowing, and not caring, if she were calling for me from behind her closed door.

When my diddy came home, he carried the Good Book in one hand and a covered basket in the other. "Everyone missed you, Del. This is for your birthday, from the Sunday's" He handed me the basket. "It's hard to believe you're twelve years old. You're growing like a weed." He took a deep breath, "How is your mother feeling?"

My heart sank at his question. I didn't know how she was feeling.

"I . . . I didn't want to disturb her . . . I never heard her call for me." He bent over and pecked my cheek with a kiss. "Go and eat, there's some fried chicken in there." He patted me on the head and made his way upstairs to check on his wife.

There was, indeed, fried chicken. There were also biscuits and fried okra and a slice of cake. After pulling out the food, I noticed a small bundle of brown paper with my name written on it. Inside was a bookmark made from braided leather strips. A birthday gift from Ida. As I spread out the paper I read the words, "I'll tell you all about it next week." A smile grew on my face.

By nightfall, my diddy had fallen asleep on the sofa in his study. Mother had made her way down for something to eat and had been sitting in the kitchen for well over an hour. I sat across from her at our table, silent, waiting to do as I was told. I had filled her glass twice and three times I sliced bread for her. She sat holding her head up with one hand as if her neck were not strong enough to do the job. I had been frightened by her before, by her anger, but never by her mere presence. But, that day there was something in her, or about her, that made me anxious.

We sat for some time even after she had finished her food. She sat, still holding her head up. I sat, still. What few guests we had that evening had long since retired to their rooms, and the house was quiet as could be. The clock that stood in the dining hall was the only noticeable sound. That is, until there came a knocking at the door.

It was faint at first. Just enough to rouse Mother to attention. The second knock was a bit louder, bringing me to my feet. "No," Mother said. "I will get the door." She stumbled to her feet and held the wall as she made her way toward the knocking.

"Mother," I started.

"This is my inn, Delitha, I can get the door."

For fear she would fall, I walked slowly behind her, hoping she would not notice me. Her feet never completely came up off the floor as she stepped. She reached out twice before gripping the doorknob. The door opened with a screech and she squinted her eyes as if the noise somehow blurred her vision. On the front porch stood a young man, a young man with the blackest skin I had ever seen. He stood holding his hat to his chest, his eyes were large, he stuttered while addressing her. "M-m-m-m . . . Ma'am. My w-w-w-wife here is, is in l-l-l-labor." He motioned to a young lady hunched over on the railing. She was pulling on her skirt and moaning to herself.

"Might y-y-y-you be s-s-s-some a-a-a-assistance?" He reached in his pocket and pulled out a coin. "I don't h-h-h-have much . . ." Before he could finish, Mother pushed her hair from her face and hissed, "I'm an innkeeper, not a midwife." She took a step back, "All our rooms are full." And with that, she closed the door in his face. She turned and tripped over me, as I was too stunned to move out of her way. "Good Lord, Delitha, are you my shadow?" She pushed at me with what little strength she had and made her way up the stairs and into her bedroom, slamming the door behind her. I could hear my diddy snoring in rhythm with the clock in the dining hall.

"The Lord is my helper, I will not be afraid," I said aloud, only moments before I ran out our front door. "Wait," I called. The couple had only made it to our gates. "I can help you, if you will let me." The young lady only smiled. The man, with tears in his eyes, answered, "T-t-t-thank you."

"Follow me," I said, taking her other arm. I led them around the house and back to the only place I could think of, to Ol' Willy.

I left them in the dark only long enough to grab a blanket, towels, and a small oil lamp. I tucked the linens under my arm and grabbed a pitcher of water from the kitchen. When I returned, the lady was already trying to lie down. I hurriedly placed the blanket beneath her.

Her legs were wider than I had expected. As she lifted her dress, it dawned on me that I had never seen another woman's body, nor had I ever seen my own from such an angle. I froze. Stared.

"D-d-d-d-do you know w-w-w-what your d-d-d-d-doin'?"

"No," I answered quietly, unable to take my eyes off the small head of hair forming between her legs.

"Do something!" The woman yelled at me, gripping her thighs. Sweat was dripping down her face like raindrops on a window. "It's comin'!" she squealed, lifting her head as though she could see this growth sliding out of her body. "Henry, oh Good God!"

Henry, whom I assumed was her husband, slid behind her and placed his knees under her head. He removed a handkerchief from his back pocket and wiped at her face. Then something unexpected happened. Henry, this man who could hardly look you in the face as he stuttered through his thoughts, began singing to his ailing wife with the smoothest of voices.

As he sang, she visibly began to relax. Her legs fell to the ground, her shoulders resting on his knees. She closed her eyes and let her mouth hang open. Henry lifted his hands high above his head into the gathering night. Suddenly, the world fell silent. The darkness overwhelmed me. I felt my body falling backwards toward the ground, and then I felt what I assumed were the hands of God catching me and leaning me against the tree trunk.

It wasn't the hand of God, at least not directly. It was my diddy's hands. He moved in between her legs and pressed his hands against her belly.

"Bear down," he said to her in his always-steady voice. "Give me some good pushes. It shouldn't take much."

Henry kept his hands raised to the heavens; he began singing even louder, now with tears streaming down his dark cheeks.

She couldn't have pressed down more than five times when this tiny, beautiful being slid from her mother's body and into my diddy's hands. She was covered in blood, and her dark, curly hair was stuck to her head. She was tiny and perfect. She made me smile, then cry. Within moments, all five of us were crying. Henry still held his hands above his head.

"What is your name, ma'am?" my diddy asked the woman as she wiped at her baby's face.

"Eloise," she answered through her laughter and tears.

"What would you like to name your daughter?"

Eloise looked up at Henry. He cradled her face in his hands and simply nodded at her.

"We'll call her Emiline."

"That's a beautiful name for beautiful little girl. Congratulations."

My diddy wrapped Emiline in a towel and laid her on her mother's chest.

Eloise unbuttoned her blouse and offered her breast to the infant. Eloise had only been in this position for a moment when she let out another cry.

"Hold on," my diddy said calmly. "You're not quite done."

To my amazement, a sac that appeared to be as large as the baby itself came oozing out onto the ground, followed by more blood and water than I had ever seen. For a moment I thought I might be sick, and I stood to move away from them. Before I could take a step, my diddy grabbed my arm with his bloody hand.

"This is an important night, Del. You have just witnessed the most amazing miracle this life has to offer." He let out a bit of laughter. "Now run inside and get another basin of water. As much as you can carry."

I ran as fast as my feet would allow, for fear of missing something. When I returned, Eloise was sitting up against Ol' Willy, holding Emiline in her arms. Henry had placed his pinky finger inside his daughter's mouth and was gently singing to her as Eloise swayed her shoulders back and forth.

It wasn't until he had finished his song that my diddy turned to me. "Wash her," he said. "Wash her and the earth, then run up and find a gown of

Mother's. I'll ride over to the theater, where I will no doubt find the doctor, I'll return as soon as I can."

"What do I . . ."

"The Lord provides wisdom when wisdom is needed, Del."

Henry took the service of cleaning his wife upon himself, and I made my way softly up the stairs to Mother's room. Her floor creaked as badly as any in the house, and I stepped across the boards on my tiptoes, trying hard not to wake her. Mother was silent. Her breathing was inaudible, and the thought crossed my mind that she might be dead. Yet, I continued on to her bureau and brought forth a white cotton nightgown. It would certainly be too long for Eloise, as she stood at least two heads shorter than Mother, but I didn't think she would mind. She seemed very kind. Besides, it seemed to me that anyone willing to follow a child under a big old weeping willow tree and then deliver their baby into the hands of stranger that crept in from behind the shadows, wouldn't complain about much of anything.

I was right. She didn't complain. Not only that, but she went on for some time about how grateful she was for our help.

"I owe a debt I can never pay," she said to me.

I only smiled back at her while running my hand over Emiline's head.

"I mean it, little one." She took my chin with her free hand and turned my face to hers. "I owe you a debt . . ." She stopped herself and looked over to her husband. They smiled at one another, Henry nodded his head. "We can pay."

"No," I said to her a bit too sternly. "You don't owe me a penny. Honest."

"A penny we don't have," she said softly. "But, one day, you'll find yourself in need, just like we found ourselves in need tonight. When that time come, if we're able, we'll help you. We'll help you the way you helped us."

Before I could respond my diddy came running from the side yard.

"If you will come with me, the doctor will meet us at his office."

"W-w-w-w-we have n-n-n-n-no m-m-m-m-oney."

"Money is of no concern. Can you lift your wife?"

Henry nodded, and while gathering the clean towels underneath her, he lifted his wife and daughter into his arms. I handed my diddy the gown to take along. Henry moved them out from the branches and followed my diddy back up to the house, then he stopped and turned to face me. "W-w-w-w-what's your n-n-n-name, l-l-l-l-little o-o-one?"

"Delitha," I answered.

"T-t-t-thank you, D-D-Delitha."

My diddy never mentioned that night again. I doubt he even told Mother. And, until now, I've never had any reason to tell. It was one of those experiences that is almost too difficult to describe, like a painting that is too beautiful for words, you simply have to see it with your own eyes; or like a heartbreak that you simply must feel for yourself to grasp the full depth of it. It was a night my diddy and I replayed often, each in our own mind. But, without being there, the story doesn't quite seem real. Therefore, we each made up our mind to simply hold it in, as the one secret night when we took part in a miracle. It turned out to a wonderful birthday after all.

The following morning seemed quite ordinary, given that it came following such an extraordinary evening. The house was rumbling with male voices; the rooms were filled with the smell of bacon and eggs and potatoes. My diddy was mingling with the men in the dining hall, exchanging pleasantries and inquiring on the business each man was in town attending to. The only great surprise for the morning was to find Mother hurrying about in the kitchen.

"Are you feeling better?"

She turned to face me, squinting at me with her bloodshot eyes. "No," she answered sharply.

"Mother, you can go back to bed. I can finish breakfast."

"Ha," she laughed to herself. "You would have this place up in flames. Go and turn down the beds."

I stood still. I wanted very badly to mind her, but my feet would not carry me away.

"Go and strip down the beds," she said again slowly, as if assuming I had not understood her the first time. Yet, my feet still would not move. Not even as she staggered toward me, bent to my height, and yelled at the top of her lungs, "GO AND STRIP DOWN THE BEDS!"

A cup and saucer clanged together in the next room. A man cleared his throat. Then there was dead silence throughout the house. My diddy appeared behind her, having made no sound. He placed one hand on her back, the other on her arm, prying her from her position two inches from my nose.

"There is no need to concern our guests," he whispered. "Beverly, darling, won't you go and lie down?" She stood tall, leaning into him a bit. She then used any amount of energy she had left to flail her right hand across my face.

It wasn't until I straightened my neck out and caught my diddy's expression that I realized she had never before struck me in front of him. This, for him, was new. He was dumbfounded. "May the Lord forgive you, Beverly," he said through his gritted teeth. "Go and lie down."

Mother walked slowly from the kitchen, supporting herself on the wall as she went. Once the kitchen door swung tight behind her, my diddy knelt and opened his arms to me. One more thing that struck me that day was that my diddy expected me to need him. In his mind, this was the first time I had ever been struck by her, a notion that broke my heart. I dove into his arms allowing him the pleasure of consoling me.

"I'm sorry, Del." He whispered into my hair. "I don't know what's wrong with her." He held me so tight it almost hurt. "I'm so sorry." His breath in my ear blocked any sound that might have been in our home that morning. Except for the sound of Mother calling his name.

"Walter!"

Her call was deafening. Her voice distorted. Unrecognizable. Blood curling. We rushed from the kitchen, as did the men from the dining hall. We all hit the foyer as she hit the stairs. She stumbled once, then rolled down as though she were a toy having been thrown by a child. Her arms flailed above her head as she rolled, knocking pictures from their nails in the wall. Her dress tangled itself around her waist exposing what bit of dignity she had left. Her body hit the floor with a thud, sending a chill down my spine. The men rushed to her, voicing their concern, but it was my diddy that gathered her up and rose above them all. He carried her up the stairs and into her room, leaving me among the men, among the giants, frightened and alone.

6

It was my favorite time of year. When the grass is at its greenest, yet it hides itself under a blanket of crisp, golden leaves. When the morning fog tricks you into thinking yours is the only house in existence. I knew, however, what hid itself in the thickness of the fog. An acre over, for instance, stood the immaculate home of the great Winston family. The estate commonly referred to as Winston Manor.

It stood a story higher than my own, with barred windows in the attic that seemed only appropriate for a prisoner. A black wrought-iron fence surrounded the home, keeping out any uninvited commoners. The house itself was quite breathtaking. Bright purple shutters contrasted the pale peach of the exterior walls. The porch, which wrapped itself around the structure, held a dozen rocking chairs, all painted the richest white. Bright green ivy twisted itself around the fence, threatening any other flower that dared grow in its direction. This is how I picture Winston Manor behind the fog when my memory is all I have to rely on.

The truth is, after the fog lifts, there is only the abandoned shell of a home, encased by the rusted wrought iron. The window boxes hold earth, but there is no life springing from it. The rocking chairs, although weathered, are still quite beautiful and in working condition. The ivy is the only piece that is true to the original picture. The estate was sold years ago to an anonymous buyer. A buyer who seems to have forgotten his purchase. My diddy says there is a family intended for every home, and perhaps this particular family is simply waiting for the appropriate time. Waiting for the Good Lord to bring them here to fulfill their purpose.

When the fog has covered the home and leaves my imagination to fill in the blanks, I picture a family with lots of children. I watch the mother sit on the porch, breaking beans with the hired hands, as the children toss a ball or run with a puppy in the front lawn. Their laughter rings in my head, as real as my own. Sometimes I am surprised that the laughter of these ghosts seems more familiar than my own.

For Mother, fall never meant more than the addition of blankets in the bedrooms. For me, this fall carried a wealth of change on its chilly breeze. Change I had not expected yet welcomed with open arms.

"Del, Del, wake up." My diddy was standing over me, whispering in my ear. He was fully dressed though the sun had barely risen. I could smell the oil from his hair. "You must get up, Del. I need your help." He crossed the room, tugging at his necktie as if it were choking him. Pulling a dress from my wardrobe, he turned and flung it onto the foot of my bed.

"I need you up and dressed. We have a guest arriving this morning at the station. You will be in charge of feeding your mother this morning, do you understand?"

"Yes, sir."

But I didn't understand. We hadn't had a guest stay in our home for months. When mother stopped making the effort to even get out of bed, we placed a NO VACANCY sign on the porch and had not had so much as a knock on the door since. Who could this guest be? I dared not ask; I could tell by the nervous shake in my diddy's voice that he only wanted to be answered, not questioned.

"I have some errands to run before heading to the station. Don't expect us back until after lunch. You should have something prepared for our dinner. Nothing fancy, but filling. She has traveled a long distance and is sure to be tired. She will want an easy meal. Do you understand?"

"Yes, sir."

"Your mother will be awake in about two hours. I have measured out her doses; they are beside her bed. If she asks for a . . ." he hesitated with an obvious frustration. "There is a bottle with brown liquid under her bed. If she asks for a drink, give her a small glass. Do not give her the bottle. Do you understand?"

"Yes, sir."

"You may not be able to leave your mother once she is awake. You must use your time wisely. Clean the room next to ours. Fresh linens; fresh water. If there are roses on the vine, cut some and fill a vase for the reading table. Open the window long enough to air the room, then shut and lock the window. Leave the curtains drawn. Do you understand?"

"Yes, sir."

He walked toward the door, then stopped and turned to look at me.

"You are the stars in my sky, Delitha." His eyes were sad. His bottom lip seemed to disappear as his jaw tightened.

"Yes, sir."

The small rosebuds were wet with dew. My fingers seemed to intentionally find every thorn. I had dressed in such a hurry that I had forgotten my shoes. The grass kissed the soles of my feet, leaving them damp and cold. The hair on my arms began to rise, and a sensation in my spine became so strong I jerked involuntarily, almost dropping the flowers.

Although I had not been instructed to, I started a small fire. The chill was irritating, and I felt this guest must be of enough importance to justify warming the room. The fireplace was small, as was the flame I created. I stood for a brief moment, rubbing my hands together, staring into the flame. Fire, like many things, could save our lives, or take them. I stood there wondering about the nature of our guest that would be arriving that day. My diddy had said *she* would have traveled a great distance. My first thought was that *she* might be a nurse, coming to help with Mother. I wondered if she were coming to save Mother's life. Little did I know she was coming to save mine.

Mother awoke precisely when diddy said she would. She did not wake with a peaceful spirit like the rest of us, feeling calm and refreshed. Instead, she disturbed the house with yelling and the flailing of her limbs. I was arranging her breakfast tray when I first heard her.

"Make them stop! Make them leave me alone!"

Her voice had become deep and raspy. Her every word held intense hostility.

"They're touching me! Why are they here? Make them go away!"

I sat her tray on the stool near the door. Although I approached her in the slow, gliding manner in which my diddy had taught me, she still flinched when she met my eyes.

"What do you want? Where's your father? Walter? Walter!"

"Mother, I have your medication. Can you sit up and I'll help you get it down."

"I don't need your help! Walter!"

"He's not here." I spoke to her as softly as I could and still be heard. "He had some errands to run. I have your medication. I have your breakfast." Her eyes were wild; she looked right through me.

"Walter! They're touching me! Please!" She buried her face in her pillow and began weeping. Her body convulsed under the blankets.

"He'll be back soon, Mother. I can make them go away, too. I can. Trust me, Mother. Let me help you, I can make them go away." She slowly began to stop crying. She turned her head showing me one eye peeking through her tousled hair.

"Can you? Can you make them leave me alone?"

"Yes, Mother. I can make them leave you alone." I cradled her in my arms for a moment, until her body began to relax.

"Can you swallow these? These are your weapons against them, Mother. These will make them go away." It was rare for me to be alone with her anymore. My diddy rarely left the house. Yet, whether I was in the room next to her bed, or in the hallway listening through the door, I always wondered the same thing. Who or what are *they*? What are these pills taking from her sight?

"I need a drink," she said, after swallowing her pills. "I need it now."

"Yes, Mother. Let me get you a glass."

"I don't need a glass, just hand me the bottle."

I found the bottle under her bed, just as my diddy had said I would. I held it up in the light; there was less than half left in the bottom. The label had been torn off, leaving me curious as to what could be so helpful and smell so terrible.

"Give it to me!" she shouted, reaching her arm above her head. Her fingernails were jagged and yellow. "Give me the damn bottle!" She pulled it from my hand and turned her back to me as she found her lips.

"No, Mother, give me that. I need to get a glass first."

I circled the bed and met her on the other side. Her grip was firm and her gaze told me she was prepared to fight for this liquid medicine. I squeezed her arm with one hand and pushed her head back with the other.

"Mother, listen to me. You shouldn't have too much of this, it could be dangerous!"

She was so thin; she looked like a child. Her cheeks were sunken in and her lips were cracked. Her eyes, once so full of life, were now dark and empty.

"Mother," I said, gently stroking her hair. "Give me the bottle."

"To hell with you!" she screamed, knocking me to the floor.

Before leaving her room, I moved her breakfast tray onto her bedside table. I hadn't made it down the stairs before I heard it hit the floor, her meal scattering like frightened mice. I gripped the banister and gritted my teeth. I didn't know her anymore. Didn't want to know her. I slapped at the tear running down my cheek, then turned my attention to the dinner preparations.

The next hour of my life was spent chopping vegetables and kneading bread. Soup, I decided, was a suitable dinner for a fall evening. The process was slow; I found myself out of practice with even holding the knife correctly. My diddy and I had been surviving on half meals and on the goodwill of the widows who missed having someone to cook for. Even though I spread a tablecloth and pulled out our better place settings, I still hesitated before setting down the third plate. My diddy and I had become accustomed to taking shifts, eating in the kitchen, trying our best to keep our cleaning chores to a minimum. The dining hall seemed unfamiliar, and the table suddenly seemed set for a family. That image, too, was unfamiliar.

I'm not certain how many times I circled the room, tugging at the tablecloth, or straightening the plates, moving them an inch or two in either direction, then back again. I placed a soup bowl in the center of each plate, then took them back to the kitchen to be washed a second time. I couldn't shake the feeling that this guest, this *she*, was of great importance. *She* consumed my thoughts. Consuming them enough that I hardly noticed the moaning and gnashing of teeth coming from the room upstairs.

When the dining hall seemed in its best condition, I made my way to the foyer, intending to peek out the front window with anticipation of my diddy's return. I never made it to the front window. When I reached the foyer, I caught my reflection in the mirror above the hall tree. My hair was untamed, my eyes held up by dark circles. My chest holding remains of my hurried breakfast. The house had been my first priority, I had given no thought to my own appearance.

"Frightful," I said aloud. "Dreadful. She'll have nothing to do with you in this condition." I examined myself for a moment longer and then darted up the stairs, skipping every other step. At the top, my foot became tangled in the hem of my dress and I tumbled to the floor outside Mother's bedroom door. I waited. "Please don't be disturbed," I whispered. But she had been disturbed. Perhaps she had dozed off, perhaps not. But the thud of my body hitting the floor was enough to alert her to the outside world.

"Walter? Is that you?"

I didn't answer.

"Walter? Where have you been? Come in here, Walter."

I had to answer her. But time was not on my side, and I desperately needed to clean myself.

"Mother?" I opened her door slowly, letting her hear my voice before seeing my face. "Mother, it's me. Diddy still isn't home. He should be arriving shortly."

She shielded her face as if the light streaming in from the hallway was painful to her eyes.

"I need your father, not you. Close the damn door."

"Mother, they'll be back soon. Can I get you something? Perhaps a glass of water?"

"They? They who? Who will be back soon?"

With that question I knew that my diddy had told Mother even less about our visitor. He had told her nothing to be exact.

I wasn't sure how to answer her.

"I asked you a question!" Her raised voice startled me.

"Diddy went to the station. He said we had a guest arriving this morning; he went to pick her up at the station."

"Her? Her who?"

"I don't know, Mother. He didn't tell me her name. I'm sorry."

She was silent for a moment. Even her breathing was inaudible. Her eyes were cast on the ceiling. She rubbed her forehead with the palms of her hands before speaking again.

"You mean your father went to the station to pick up a woman, and he's bringing her here?"

"Yes, ma'am."

She tucked her hands under her hips and brought herself to a sitting position. Then she began rubbing her forehead again.

"Your father went to the station to pick up a woman, he's bringing her here, and he didn't tell you her name?"

"Yes, ma'am."

She let out a deep sigh before saying, "Let me be."

I tiptoed across the hall and into my own room. The first order of business was my hair. It was a tangled mess, far more snarled than usual, and the force it took to clear the tangles brought forth tears. I tried several different styles before allowing the locks to simply rest on my shoulders, revealing my temples by pulling back the sides with pins.

"That's better," I thought, pinching my cheeks to add a bit of color. Next was my dress. Diddy had handed me one more suitable for spring. I replaced it with a simple brown skirt, one long enough to hide the hole in my stockings, and an off-white blouse. As I sat down to lace my boots, I felt the morning's activities take a toll on my body. If I simply blinked, my eyes did not want to reopen. My heart seemed to be beating a bit faster than normal, yet my body seemed to be moving in slow motion.

As I sat, exhausted, I began surveying my room. The floor had not been swept in weeks; there was dust standing on every flat surface. Then, I remember noticing the size of my room, perhaps for the first time. Mine was the smallest in the house, yet it was large enough for at least three more beds, probably more. I looked around my room that day wishing I had a sister, or a brother. Several of each would have been fine. I wished my diddy were bringing home playmates for me rather than this mystery lady that would likely be stuffy and boring, like most women who stayed with us. It was a shame, I thought, that my grandfather only had one son, and that he married a lady that could only give him one daughter. My father's only sister had never married, so there were no cousins to come and visit. There would be no nieces or nephews through the years for me to gush over. It was a shame, I thought, that we were given this house, rather than a family overrun with children. I believed my diddy when he said that every house has a family intended for it, and every family has a purpose to fulfill in that house. Yet, once the decision was made to close the inn, I couldn't help but wonder what our purpose was. Or perhaps what our purpose would become. It seemed, in my mind at least, that we were wasting away in this great big house, and the world was turning 'round without us.

I stood, with good intentions of finding a rag to dust my room. When I entered our pantry, I heard the motorcar pull up in front of our house. I hurried to the front window, excited by the rumbling of the motor. I watched my diddy step out of the motorcar. He stopped, looked around, then reached inside the car again as if he had forgotten something. The first part of her I saw was her white glove, resting on my diddy's arm. She emerged from her seat and immediately opened her umbrella. It was also white, as was her hat, dress, and shoes. She looked like an angel, shining amongst the colors of nature. They took a step forward, away from the car, and she stopped. She repositioned her umbrella and that is when I saw it. The mole under her mouth. It was the same *she* from grandfather's funeral. Excitement paralyzed me. I was about to meet the mystery woman. This *she* looked up at the house then looked at me in the front window. She was magnificent.

7

My heart was racing, and I stood frozen in my shoes. They walked leisurely to the porch, as if enjoying my sudden anxiety. Then I heard their footsteps on the wooden steps, and the click of the door as the knob turned. They entered slowly; her umbrella was first into the room. I could feel my heart in my throat, and I felt as if I might faint. "Delitha, I presume." Her voice was as splendid as her presence.

I couldn't move. I couldn't speak. I was in complete awe of this *She*.

"Del," my diddy said, breaking the silence, "this is your Aunt . . ."

"Esther," came a booming voice from above us.

We all looked up to see who had finished my diddy's sentence, as if we didn't recognize the voice. Mother was standing on the balcony, the entire weight of her body resting on the banister.

"Well, look what the cat dragged in," Mother hissed.

"Hello, Beverly."

"Beverly," my diddy's voice seemed to echo through our house. "Esther will only be staying with us for a short time."

"How wonderful," she said leaning daringly over the edge of the balcony, causing my diddy to take a step forward. "Although I don't remember sending an invitation."

"Enough!" Diddy stomped his foot on the floor. A clump of hair fell from its mold and flopped against his forehead.

"Delitha, take your Aunt Esther to the kitchen," he said, placing his hand on her back, "I'm sure she could use some tea."

"Yes, sir."

I began to walk away when my Aunt Esther, whom I had never met, took my hand and led me. I looked up at her in surprise, and she simply winked at me with one of her large brown eyes. I saw my diddy out of the corner of my eye, flying up the stairs. Their voices were muffled, but I could hear the argument as he forced Mother back to her room.

"If you don't have tea prepared, water will be fine; I'm not fussy." She sat at the kitchen table and removed her hat and gloves. Her hair was pinned in a loose bun on the back of her head. Tiny strands had escaped and stood from the bunch, waving with her movement. After settling herself, she began smoothing her hair with her elegant, bare hands. I placed two glasses of water and a small plate of sliced cheese and crackers between us, then seated myself directly across from her.

"I apologize for . . ."

"Child," she interrupted, "there's not a thing in this world for you to apologize for." She winked at me again, taking a bite of cheese. "Your father tells me you are doing quite well with your studies. What is your favorite subject?"

"I'm good with my numbers, I suppose."

"Oh, that's wonderful. I knew the moment I saw your face that you were very smart."

I felt myself blushing.

"Spelling? Are you good with your vocabulary?"

"Yes, ma'am. I suppose I am."

"That's wonderful. Is your father teaching you French at all?"

"No, ma'am."

"Now, that is a shame. What a beautiful language."

She spoke with such animation; it was difficult not to smile while watching her. Not a smile to hide a snicker, but a smile of pleasure. Her voice was upbeat, pleasant to the ear. Her tone was steady and cheerful. She displayed something I couldn't put my finger on, yet it was something I immediately wanted for myself.

"Well, I shouldn't be asking you all these questions. You probably have questions for me, don't you?"

I didn't answer, lost in her spell.

"For instance, you're probably wondering why you've never met me before. Am I right? Well, as you heard in there," she jerked her head toward the door, "your mother is not exactly fond of me. Why? Well, that's a different story for a different day, but let me assure you that your father and I are on the best of terms. I've thought of you often, and were I a better person, I would have picked up my pen and written you a letter. Shame on me, Delitha. I am truly sorry for not reaching out to you until now."

She stopped for a breath and a sip of her water.

"Of course, your father is no help at all, the foolish man." She began looking around the room. "How long has the telephone been available? Long enough I tell you. Long enough for me to have had two installed and your father refuses to be a part of the modern world. I'm still in shock that he replaced his horse drawn carriage." She smiled at me. "Your father is an old soul." She put extra emphasis on the word old. "Go ahead, ask me something. Anything, anything at all. You see I'm one of those people that can't stand silence. If you don't say something, I'll be forced to continue telling you everything that's on my mind. And, at some point, I promise, you'll think me a bore."

I wanted to laugh out loud. She had only been in my presence for a matter of minutes and already I felt a giddiness in my soul that I had forgotten existed.

"Where have you traveled from?" I asked her, trying hard to keep my voice steady.

"What a wonderful question. I live in New York, a wonderful city. I think you would really love it there."

"I imagine so," I said, shuffling my feet under the table. "But, I don't expect to ever see such a place. It's so far away."

"It is far away, you're right about that much."

"Are you ladies getting acquainted?" My diddy entered the room with a burst of energy and squeezed his sister's shoulders. "Esther, it is so good to have you here."

She placed her hands on his. "Oh, darling. I have missed you so. You told me Delitha was smart, but you failed to mention her beauty. She favors our mother, don't you think?"

They both stared at me for a moment, and Aunt Esther let out a sigh. "It is such a shame that families can't be together forever. A terrible shame."

"Ah, sister, have you learned nothing in all your years?" he circled the table and took a seat next to me. "We will be together forever. This world is not our home. We will meet those who have gone on before us and we will live together. Forever."

She smiled at him for several seconds, then she began shaking her finger at him. Your father is a wise man. Stubborn, but wise. I think we shall keep him. Do you agree?"

She rose from the table, gathering her gloves and hat. She picked up another piece of cheese and placed it on a cracker. "Ah, my darlings, I am very fond of afternoon naps. I hope my laziness does not offend you."

"Oh, Esther," my diddy said, "make yourself at home here. You sleep, eat, and sleep again at your own liking." He circled the table again and embraced her. She kissed him on the cheek, then looked my way.

"I hear you have prepared my room, Delitha. I do thank you. Even before I see it, I sense you took extra care to make my stay here a pleasant one." She blew me a kiss. "I'll look forward to seeing you for dinner."

My diddy escorted her up the stairs and into her room. His footsteps were heavier than usual as he carried her bags. My Aunt Esther reclined in her room. My diddy escaped to his study. Mother lay brewing in her bed, and I was left alone with a plate of cheese, crackers, and nothing to do but think.

Why on earth had she come here now? I doubted that she had come to assist Mother. After all, diddy had said she would only be here for a short time. Had diddy known she was coming? Why had he not mentioned her arrival before? Why was mother not pleased to see her? Why had she come? My mind was racing with questions, and there were no answers to be given. My anticipation of a nursemaid had given me hope that Mother would be recovering. Though I felt disappointment, there was also excitement in my heart. Aunt Esther had only just arrived, yet I could not remember the last time I had felt such joy from another person. Her joy seemed to seep from her pores, infecting everything around her. Dinner could scarcely come soon enough, but finally, it did.

She was truly magnificent. Perhaps it was the way she blew on her spoon before every bite. Or, perhaps it was the way she raised her pinky finger as she sipped her tea. Whatever the reason, I simply could not keep my eyes off her. It felt so wonderful to laugh out loud. I even caught my diddy covering his mouth to keep his food in while his laughter rang out. Our conversation was easy, natural. I had never seen anyone like her. There was a spark about her that was contagious. She spoke quickly and precisely. She demanded attention. Aunt Esther told us stories of life in the city, and of the strange people that fill its streets. She complimented our dinner, and said a simple bowl of soup was so refreshing.

"Lillian insists on preparing lamb, or veal, and every dish comes with potatoes," she said. "She is trying to fatten me up, I tell you. And I fear it is working."

My diddy chuckled, "You mean Lillian is still putting up with you?"

"Who is Lillian?" I asked, chuckling along with my diddy.

"Lillian is your Aunt Esther's maid," my diddy answered, "and obviously the most patient human being on the face of the earth."

"Very funny." Aunt Esther teasingly slapped at him, in a way I'd seen Ida slap at her brothers. "She is very patient, indeed. However, I have never referred to Lillian as my maid. She is my very best friend and she enjoys . . . putting up with me." She slapped at my diddy again and they exchanged large toothy grins.

"Oh, I don't think it would be hard to put with you," I said. "I think you're perfect."

"You are such a charmer," she said, leaning forward. "Tell me, have you charmed any of the young men in the area?" I glanced up at my diddy and was suddenly reminded of my youth. Aunt Esther, in all her glory, had momentarily convinced me that I was an equal. An adult attending a dinner party. A celebration in honor of a loved one returning home for an overdue visit. It was the way he looked at me that brought my mind back to its true self. He looked at me as only a father could. He looked at me with eyes that silently apologized for robbing me of the life he knew I wanted. The life he felt I deserved.

"There hasn't been much time for that sort of business, has there?"

"No, sir," I replied.

"Well, now. There's no hurry in that department," Aunt Esther spoke directly to me as if she knew the war that was taking place inside my heart. It was as if she knew I had been drug back to reality and she was trying with her voice to lure me back to the fantasy. "You know, you are a lady now, Delitha. The world is changing. The expectations of a woman are changing. You just remember that you control your charm. Enjoy being a lady before you go and give yourself away." She leaned back in her chair, "I dare not tell you my age, but even I have yet to give myself away." She smiled sheepishly. "I admit it. I have yet to charm the heart of a good man."

"Ah, Esther. There have been plenty of suitors," Diddy said, resting his arm on the back of my chair. "The truth is, you are as picky as they come. Believe you me, there have been many a man charmed by your good spirit."

"I never said I hadn't charmed a man. I said I had never charmed a good man." She reached for my hand from across the table. "Patience is key when it comes to matters of the heart. The one you give your heart to can change the very course of your life. Isn't that right, brother?"

He held her gaze briefly before wiping his mouth and scooting back from the table.

"Del, this was a fine meal. If you ladies will excuse me, I need to attend to my wife." He stood and kissed me on the forehead. "Perhaps you will come bid your Mother goodnight before you turn in."

"Yes, sir."

"May I help you clear the table?" Aunt Esther asked as she stood, still holding her teacup.

"No, ma'am. We never allow our guests to help with the housework."

"I am not a guest. I'm family. Besides, Lillian treats me as though I'll break if I so much as lift a finger. I would very much enjoy helping you." She picked up her plate and bowl and reached for my diddy's. "Not to mention the fact that I simply love your company. It's worth washing dishes to simply be with you."

I felt myself blush again.

"Come now. Let's get these dishes washed, and then you can show me what's worth seeing around here."

She moved around the kitchen like a lost puppy. We bumped into one another a number of times before she finally laughed at herself and leaned against the wall. "Well, how obvious is it that I spend very little time in the kitchen? Well, that isn't true; I eat in the kitchen every single day, but I don't make it past the table." She let out a nervous laugh. "I confess I couldn't even tell you the color of the wallpaper in my kitchen. For that matter, I'm not sure that there is wallpaper in my kitchen."

I glanced at the walls that surrounded us, plum colored, scattered flowers; Mother had always loved the pattern. One of the few things I knew for certain that she loved.

"Mother says I have no need to learn French because I will never travel Europe. But, I need to learn my kitchen because I will always need to eat."

Aunt Esther put her hands behind her back and smiled at me.

"Perhaps your mother is wiser than I thought." She pushed herself from the wall and took the saucers from my hands. "Where do these go?"

I pointed, rather than telling her. Her eyes followed my finger and she slowly moved in that direction, the smile never leaving her face.

"Perhaps you could teach me to prepare something. Lillian would really get a kick out of that."

"What would you like to learn?"

"Oh, well, your father says you make a wonderful apple strudel. How about that?" She placed the saucers in their spot and before I could answer, she gasped and swung around to look at me.

"Oh, dear. Will you look at that! I've broken a fingernail. There'll be no hiding this from Lillian, she inspects me like a prison guard."

"Why do you keep her on? She sounds like a pest," I giggled, latching the cupboard.

"Have you ever loved to hate someone?" she hesitated, then waved her hand as if waving away the question.

"Oh, Lillian has been with us for as long as I can remember. She practically raised your father and I. She looked after both our parents until they passed on, and then she insisted on staying with me." She smiled at me with a devilish smile.

"I've fired her several times, but she just won't leave. She'll never quit and she's much too stubborn to die. I do believe I'm stuck with her." She bent down to look me in the eye. "She would just adore you. Lillian makes the best chocolate cake you've ever tasted. She makes Swedish meatballs you would sell your birthright for." She stood and placed her hands on her hips.

Suddenly there was a loud noise from the room above us, as if someone had fallen. Then there were loud footsteps above our heads. We stood still, staring up at the ceiling. Then came the yelling. Mother's voice was at its peak. Although I couldn't make out her words, I knew they were full of anger. What I didn't know at the time, was that my diddy was breaking the same news to Mother that Aunt Esther would soon be breaking to me.

"What can you show me?" she asked, forcing my eyes off the ceiling. "I imagine every room in this house looks much like the one I'm staying in. Is there a place you go to be alone, where you hide from the world? A place just for you that no one else knows of?"

"Yes, ma'am. But, diddy might need my help . . ."

"Delitha," she interrupted, "your father can handle her." Her voice was stern, yet her eyes remained soft.

I led her out to Ol' Willy. She walked with her hands falling freely by her side unlike myself, fiddling with my fingers and picking at their tips. When we reached Ol' Willy, she stood looking up at him, smiling to herself. To my surprise, she gave no thought to her white dress, sitting down on the bare earth alongside of me. "This is perfect," she whispered. "Much like the retreat of my younger days. We have a lot in common, you and I."

I couldn't hide my smile. I couldn't calm my heart. Although we sat silently for quite some time, I felt as though I were sitting with an old friend. Not an aunt I had just met. There were no need for words. We sat listening to the wind whirl around us, admiring the deep blue sky that would soon turn to winter gray. Ol' Willy's thinning branches seemed to embrace us, shielding us as best it could from the chill. I wondered how Aunt Esther knew to ask of my secret place. She broke the silence, answering my question before I could ask.

"You know, everyone has a refuge. Even if it's simply inside one's own head. But, the great ones . . . they have a haven. This haven is perfect." She took and squeezed my hand. Her lips looked larger in the moonlight. Shadows cast themselves all around us. Her entire being appeared larger than life. She seemed to glow. Her skin was pale. Radiant. Her hands were small, with long fingers. Her nails were painted the color of her lips, her cheeks a shade lighter. I felt proud that her blood was in my veins, that I carried her name. For a moment, my mind wondered back to Aunt Esther's arrival and the few words she exchanged with Mother. I felt anger building in me as I remembered the look on Mother's face when their eyes met. How could Mother have been so rude? What about this perfect being could Mother not love? She was jealous, I decided. Mother was jealous of her beauty and her wit. Mother didn't deserve a friend like Aunt Esther. Mother didn't deserve . . .

"Delitha," Aunt Esther broke my train of thought, tugging on my hand, bringing it to her lap. "You are hardly a child. I know you can see that your mother's condition has worsened."

"Yes, ma'am."

"Your father has put his whole heart into caring for your mother, but there is little he can do for her now." Her face became more serious, yet her touch remained tender. "Your father has found a hospital that can help her. Or at least they want to try. He will be taking her there on Monday."

I knew her condition had worsened, but not to the extent of finding a hospital. I suddenly felt very childish and naïve.

"Will you be going with us?" I asked trying to sound nonchalant.

"No. This journey is for your parents, and for them alone." She moved back as to look me square in the eye. "Your father will be staying with her. Do you understand what I'm telling you?"

"Have you come here to stay with me? Until Mother is able to come home?"

"No, child," she hesitated, brushing my hair from my eyes. "I've come to take you home with me."

The moment the words left her mouth, my lip began to quiver and tears welled up in my eyes.

"Oh, Delitha. I know it will be hard at first. At any point that you want to come home, I'll do my best to . . ."

Before she could finish, I lunged at her, wrapping my arms tight around her neck. We shifted back against Ol' Willy's trunk and she gasped as I pressed my cheek to hers. "Thank you," I whispered. "Thank you."

8

On Sunday, my diddy said goodbye to his people, his flock.

"The Good Lord did not say when we would return," he told us, "only that we must go."

He spoke to the congregation as if speaking to a classroom of children, reassuring us that our needs would be met.

"Brother Holland," he told us, "will uplift your hearts and fill you with a joy perhaps you didn't know you lacked. He will provide for you just as the Good Lord has provided for you, by bringing this fine young man our way." Perhaps only I could hear the quivering in his voice. Perhaps only I saw the redness in his cheeks. Perhaps only the Good Lord saw Ida holding my hand beneath our hymnal.

"I don't understand why you have to leave; and all the way to New York City." Ida walked in small circles as she spoke. She had led me outside as soon as we were dismissed. "Besides the fact that I'm eaten up with jealousy that you're going to New York City and I'm not . . . I'm also in denial that I'm losing my best friend." She planted her hands on her hips as if she were scolding me.

"You're not losing me," I assured her. "I'll only be gone for . . . well, I'm not sure for how long, but it can't be forever. I mean, they'll have Mother fixed up in no time, and then I'll come home and everything will be just as it was."

"No it won't," she whined. "Nothing will be the same while you're gone, and nothing will be the same when you return."

"We'll write, every day if we can. I swear, Ida. New York is just another place where I'll eat, sleep, and breathe. New York will not replace you."

She looked to the earth and began shuffling tiny stones between her feet.

"That person you're always looking for . . ." She placed her hand over my heart. "New York is the place where you'll find her. And I won't be there to help her come out." Ida's eyes drifted over my shoulder and rested on something I could not see. "She's beautiful, your Aunt Esther. She's going to turn you into a lady. *She* is my replacement."

Ida's eyes returned to mine as the tears spilled onto her cheeks. She smiled her Miss America smile and began to laugh. "I'm really going to miss you Delitha Susan Viney Missy Leigh." I held my breath as she wrapped her arms around me, squeezing with all her might. I would miss her too. I would miss her terribly; there was no denying it. Yet, I had spent my entire life missing a life I had never known, and the possibility of that life meeting me on the other end of the tracks was almost more than I could bear.

"Delitha, we need to get going." Her voice rang in my ears like music, my favorite song, *my* medicine. "Delitha, your father is already in the car." I turned, letting her know I had heard her. I turned again to face Ida. I opened my mouth but nothing came out. There was nothing more to say. Words were unnecessary. I began to step backwards, away from Ida. As I raised my hand to blow her a kiss, she turned and ran before my fingers ever met my lips.

I was to travel by train, Mother by car. Although our destinations were different, it was assumed we would both return . . . better. Better people. Better spirited. Healthier. Happier. Our goodbyes were short. My diddy cupped my face in his hands and kissed my forehead.

"The time has come for you to kneel and talk with the Lord on your own. Promise me you will do this." I stood, looking at a man I had looked at every day of my life, and only then did I notice how tired he was. That he was aging. That he was sad. That no matter how often he was found on his knees, he doubted.

"I promise," I told him. I kissed his cheek and felt his stubble as I moved away.

Mother was sleeping when I entered her room to say goodbye. I did not wake her, for fear of sending her into fits. I did touch her. I stroked her arm, an arm that was once smooth and milky-white, now yellowed and textured. She frightened me. She infuriated me. But at that moment, she freed me. I tiptoed from her room that day certain of nothing. Hoping in everything. I reopened her door and whispered, "Thank you." It was all I could think to say. It was, after all, her pain that had brought my peace.

****

New York was like a dream. The buildings were like mountains towering over us. The streets were chilled from the permanent shadow. There were more cars than I had ever seen. More people too, for that matter. There was more activity in my line of sight, than in the entire town of Savannah on the Fourth of July. Tiny stores lined the streets, and as we passed by, there seemed to be someone coming or going from every single one of them. I couldn't help but hold my breath, nor could I help but smile.

"What do you think?" Aunt Esther asked, taking my hand.

"I had no idea such a place existed," squeezing her hand back as I answered.

She laughed to herself and quickened her pace. It took two of my hurried steps to match her one long stride. Her legs moved under her dress as if she were floating. She was strong, yet soft and sleek. She seemed to sparkle in the sunshine, reminding me of the horse, Sterling, that Ida's father rode. Sterling had come to Ida's father as wild as a bobcat. Mr. Sunday worked with him every day, slowly taming him. You could look into Sterling's eyes even now and see a hint of that wild colt. That is what I saw in Aunt Esther. She was a gentlewoman, yet there was strength and resistance in everything she did.

"Where are all these people going?" I asked.

"Oh, who knows. Work, home, to buy groceries." She looked down at me and squinted her eyes. "The people here are no different from the people in Savannah."

"There are just more of them," I replied.

"Will you wait here for me, darling?" She stopped abruptly and pointed to a bench on the sidewalk. "Sit there, will you? I'll only be a moment."

"Can I not come with you?"

"What, and spoil the surprise?" She brushed my cheek with her forefinger. "I'll be right back. Sit tight, darling."

In an instant, she had faded into the crowd. The only soul I knew in this city had just walked away from me. Yet, I never questioned whether or not she would return. I felt as natural there on that busy sidewalk as I had in my own bedroom. It was wonderful. The people, the noises, the smells . . . all passed by me like a parade. I just sat and smiled, taking it in, etching every detail into my memory for fear that it all might up and vanish. For all I knew, I was still fast asleep on the train, and I would soon wake to find myself elsewhere. And there was nowhere else I wanted to be. Nowhere on earth could I imagine there being a place more spectacular than this. I remember giggling aloud with excitement, and quickly covering my mouth for fear that someone had seen me. And someone had.

"You'll sleep tonight, there's no question about that!" Aunt Esther sang in her sweet voice. She handed me a small handful of roses. "These are for you. Welcome to New York."

"Oh, Aunt Esther, thank you. This is all so . . ." I couldn't find the words to describe what I was seeing or feeling. It was all I knew of falling in love.

"Come, dear. Lillian is waiting; she's dying to meet you."

"Are you certain she'll like me?"

"Are you serious? She's going to wrap you up and keep you in her pocket." We exchanged a chuckle. "I'll bet she's been baking all morning. And the first thing she'll say to you is that she's got to put some meat on your bones, and then she'll usher you into the kitchen and you'll spend the entire afternoon taste testing all her treats." She smiled, took my hand and with a quick nod of her head, she said, "Let's go home."

Home was something I had not given much thought to. Home, meaning the physical house I would be staying in. We stopped in front of a cement staircase that led up to a wide door that had been painted the same shade as the trunk of Ol' Willy.

"Here we are," Aunt Esther said looking down at me.

I literally gasped. "Why are all the houses stuck together?" I asked. "Where is your yard, don't you have a yard?"

Aunt Esther let out a burst of laughter.

"It is a bit different from what you're used to. But, I do think you'll be comfortable here." She looked me in the eye. "There is a bit of grass in the back. You can do with it what you wish." She pointed down the long street. "There is a beautiful park not too far from here. We can visit anytime."

"Wait a minute!" I exclaimed, turning a full circle. "We left our bags at the station. I was so excited . . . I left all my . . ."

"No dear, Carlton will be bringing them. We didn't forget them."

"Carlton?"

"Carlton is my driver. He will bring our bags shortly. I just thought after sitting for so long, you might enjoy the walk, and I didn't think we would want to carry your trunk all this way."

"Will he be here before . . ."

"Oh, here he is now," she said, waving.

A shiny black Ford rolled up and parked just inches away from where we stood on the sidewalk.

"Afternoon, ma'am," Carlton said as he stepped from the car. Although he stood a head shorter than Aunt Esther, he was very broad, very strong.

"I'll unload your bags, ma'am. Have them inside shortly."

"Thank you, Carlton." She took my hand, "This is Delitha, she will be staying with us for a while."

"Good to meet you, miss."

Aunt Esther squeezed my hand.

"Thank you," I whispered.

Aunt Esther turned to go up the stairs when I heard a deep, raspy voice that directed my eyes to the front door. "Good heavens, don't just stand there . . . git yourselves inside."

I looked up at Aunt Esther. In my own way, I suppose I was asking permission. She simply nodded and I found myself running up the steps and right into the arms of a stranger.

"Our Georgia Peach has arrived," she said, holding me at arm's length. "Let me look at'cha." She examined me from top to bottom. "The first thing we need to do is git some meat on those bones." She took my chin in her hand and kissed my forehead. "Follow me."

Aunt Esther's home was like nothing I had ever seen. Grand was the only word that came to mind and everything glistened as if it had been freshly polished.

"Keep movin," Lillian called to me. "I've been cookin' all mornin' and I expect you to eat it up!" I turned to follow this short, round woman with Aunt Esther at my heels, smiling. We passed an open staircase leading to rooms I couldn't wait to discover. Past the dining room was a small swinging door leading to the kitchen. I was overwhelmed by the sweetness in the air as I entered.

"Lillian, my goodness. You have been cooking all morning!" Aunt Esther removed her gloves and hat. She winked at me as she placed them on the countertop.

There was a table in the center of the room; Lillian pulled out a chair for me and I sat, without thinking. Before me lay a feast I could only have dreamed of. There was a large baked ham, sweet potatoes, beans, rolls with jam, ice tea, and four different types of dessert.

"Dessert is the most important part!" Lillian exclaimed. "Dig in."

She placed a plate before Aunt Esther and me and then stood back grinning from ear to ear. She took the roses from my hand and replaced them with a fork.

"Lillian, really. You didn't have to go to all this work." She leaned in to me and smiled. "Although she is worth it, don't you think?"

"Yes, ma'am. Sweet as pie," Lillian answered. "Now, hush up and eat."

"Yes, ma'am," Aunt Esther and I said in unison.

I cleared my plate within minutes and Lillian gave me a sample of each dessert she had created. She proudly announced, "There's chocolate cake, strawberry tart, lemon custard and my favorite, homemade vanilla ice cream."

Aunt Esther accepted a slice of chocolate cake with a small scoop of the vanilla ice cream and she smiled with each bite, not taking her eyes off me.

"Where will I be sleeping?" I finally had the nerve to ask.

"Upstairs, dear. Would you like to see your room?"

"Very much," I answered, slurping down the last swallow of the ice cream. "Thank you, Lillian. This was delicious."

"You are more than welcome, Sunshine." She handed me back my roses; she had placed them in a ceramic vase with water. Her eyes twinkled as I thanked her.

As we exited the kitchen, something caught my eye. It was a large, brown box hanging on the wall. "Tell me you've at least seen a telephone," Aunt Esther exclaimed, placing her hands on my shoulders.

"No ma'am," I said, unable to remove my eyes from this box that held endless possibilities.

"Well, then. Tomorrow we shall call . . . someone. We can't have you not knowing how to use the darn thing."

"My diddy says telephones will make us lazy. That good penmanship is important."

"Well," was all she could think to say.

Aunt Esther and I had made it up the staircase when she stopped and turned to me. She gestured towards the first door and said, "This is your room, dear. I desperately hope you like it. It was designed with the charm of a twelve year old girl in mind."

As the door opened and the room came into full view, I felt as though I had just become a princess. The bed was covered in all white linens. There were more pillows than I could count, of all different shapes and sizes. There was a porcelain china doll propped up in the center. She wore a green dress with tiny white flowers and a white lace collar. On her yellow hair sat a brown hat with a red flower pinned to the side. Her cheeks were as rosy as her lips and her eyes as brown as her hat.

On my vanity sat a brush and mirror that looked as though I would be the first to use them. There was a pair of pink slippers next to the stool on the floor. In the corner was a large plush chair with a side table covered in books and small vases of fresh flowers. Floral paintings hung sporadically around the room and they seemed to glow in the light coming through the window. The white curtains had been pulled and were tied back with pink ribbon.

Aunt Esther took a deep, cleansing breath. "I have a gown for you to sleep in. We can unpack your bags in the morning. Are you tired?"

I simply shook my head. Sleep was the last thing on my mind.

"I know this has all been very exciting but you really should try and sleep."

Before I could respond, Lillian came in with a water pitcher and basin. She set it on a small table next to the vanity. She had a long, white cotton nightgown draped over her arm.

"Wash up before you git into bed. Don't want to turn those white sheets brown overnight." She smiled at me and gently placed the gown on my bed. "I'll be back to tuck you in shortly," Aunt Esther said, kissing my forehead.

I was left standing in the center of the room, my heart still racing with excitement. I had decided over supper that, if it were all a dream, I would try hard to never wake up. I circled the room and traced my fingers along every stitch and groove before stopping to wash my hands and face. The water was cool and refreshing. I tossed the water up on my face in small quick strokes.

For an instant, I found myself back in the pond with Ida. When my eyes opened again, I couldn't help but smile at where I really was.

The gown Aunt Esther had for me was a size too large. Yet, I couldn't bring myself to complain; instead, I folded the sleeves at the cuff and reminded myself to lift the bottom up as I walked. Miss Annie, which is the name I gave to my new doll, sat up in bed next to me.

"It's a shame you can't feel how soft these sheets are," I said to her, removing her hat for a more comfortable night's sleep. The room, my room, was large. Large enough that I remember feeling very small lying there in the middle of it all.

"You look like my mother," Aunt Esther said as she entered my room. "I'm certain you'll be hearing that a lot from me. I miss her dreadfully."

She crossed the room and sat on the edge of my bed. "She was a good woman. I wish you could have known her. I wish a lot of things . . . " she trailed off, lost in her own world. A clock in the hallway chimed and brought her back to me.

"I'm right across the hall if you need me. But, I know you'll be fine." She began tucking the bedding up around my chest. As she stood, she spoke to me over her shoulder. "I'm looking forward to your stay here. Lillian and I both." At the door she paused and turned to me. "I know your parents will miss you, I'm certain you'll hear from them soon." As she closed the door I heard her whisper, "Sweet dreams."

"Aunt Esther," I called, before the door was latched.

"Yes, dear?"

"There's no wallpaper in your kitchen. It's been painted the palest of blues."

Although I was filled to the rim with sugar, it wasn't long before my eyes began to feel heavy. My blinks lasted longer and longer. My breathing became effortless. I slept steadily, well into the night, until Mother began haunting my dreams. I could see her lying in a strange bed, frightened and alone. Yet, she was only alone in her mind. My diddy was there with her, sitting by her side, also feeling frightened and alone, unable to calm her. I could see her wrenching under her covers, screaming into the night. I heard her as if she were lying next me.

I woke with a start, covered in sweat with a stabbing pain in my gut. It was then that I realized I was the one who was alone. I knew Aunt Esther was across the hall, but it would hurt my pride too much to go crawling into her arms so soon. I had only just arrived and I did not want her looking at me as a victim. As a scared little girl.

"I will survive this night," I told myself. "I will." I told Miss Annie. Pulling the covers high above my head, I began rocking back and forth, holding myself, trying to imagine I was home in my own bed with my diddy across the hall, not an aunt I had only just met.

As my efforts failed, the pain in my gut became more brutal. Tossing the covers to my feet, I looked around the room frantically. The instant I spotted the basin under my water pitcher, I darted from my bed and grabbed it. I placed the basin at my feet and hunkered over it like a kitten ready to lap up warm milk. Pulling my hair back with one hand and gripping my gown with the other, I began filling the basin with all the wonderful food Lillian had spent the day preparing.

This is how I remember my first night in Aunt Esther's home. I cried, and heaved, and cried some more. When my stomach was empty, I sat at the edge of my bed, shaking and cold. When there were no more tears, no more shivers, no more life left in me, I fell backwards and let the exhaustion take me over.

After hours of what seemed like nonexistence, I was wakened by a warm sensation on my legs. I opened my eyes to find Lillian standing over me.

"Good heaven's child." She too had her attention on my legs. I jumped from the bed so quickly that I lost my balance and tumbled to the floor.

"I'm sorry," I whimpered, "I'm so sorry. I didn't mean to wet the bed. I'm so sorry." My tears were coming out as quickly as my words. "I'm so sorry."

"Miss Esther!" Lillian yelled toward the open door.

"Please don't tell Aunt Esther!" I pleaded. "She'll be angry with me!"

"Don't be silly, child. There's nothing here to be angry about."

"Is there a problem?" Aunt Esther asked, rushing in the door.

Lillian didn't answer. She simply nodded toward the bed sheets then to the basin on the floor.

"Oh, Delitha." She began walking toward me with what I thought was a look of disappointment.

"I'm so sorry." I flinched out of habit and covered my face with both hands.

"You have nothing to apologize for," she spoke softly, quietly. "Come to me."

I slowly peeled my hands from my face, but my body was shaking again. Aunt Esther came toward me, slowly, with her hands out as if approaching a wild animal. When I caught my reflection in the vanity's mirror, I realized that is exactly how I appeared. My hair was tangled and tossed around on my head. Darkness circled my eyes. The color had fled from my cheeks and my lips were chapped and cracked, exposing small bits of dried blood.

"I look like her," I said to myself. "I look like Mother."

My head began shaking in disbelief and I frantically began combing at my hair. "Delitha, stop. Please stop." Aunt Esther was before me on her knees, wrapping her arms around my waist, pulling me into her. "Please stop."

I remember believing her; believing that she wasn't angry and that there was nothing to apologize for. Her arms were warm and safe. I could feel the love she had for me. Yet, despite my best efforts, I couldn't stop myself. It was as if I had no control over my movements, over the sounds coming from within. For the first time in my life, I was out of control. Not Mother, not my life, but me. *I* was out of control.

Aunt Esther remained on her knees, pleading with me to please stop. As my head shook from side to side I could see Lillian standing, covering her mouth with her hands. Tears running down her cheeks. And it wasn't until I felt the warmth of Aunt Esther's tears that my body began to calm itself. My movements became slower; my groaning became more shallow until finally I felt myself collapse.

I expected myself to hit the floor. My body felt like a heavy brick and the fall from my stance to Aunt Esther's chest felt like the plunge of death. My body hit hers like a stone being cast from an angry mob. But, she did not falter. She did not move. She caught me and held me until I made the first move to separate our bodies.

"There are no worries," she said to me, smoothing my hair from my face. With a forced smile she said, "Help me strip the bed while Lillian draws you a bath." And with no direct order, Lillian hurried from the room and down the hall. I heard the water hitting the porcelain tub, splashing against the sides like a rainstorm. I heard Lillian sniffle and blow her nose. I heard Aunt Esther sigh. The clock chimed out in the hallway. I could hear Mother telling me that all I do is cause trouble.

I stood, watching Aunt Esther strip my bed. She had asked for my help, but did not correct me when I stood still watching her clean up my mess. The sheets hit the floor with a swish and I heard Aunt Esther's necklace click against her chest as she approached me. Taking my hand, she led me to the bathroom. She led me there and handed me over to Lillian.

The room smelled warm. There was a slight steam hovering above the tub. The mirror was fogged over. The floor was damp. Lillian moved behind me and tugged at my soiled gown.

"Arms up," she said in an almost whisper.

As my gown came over me and fell to the floor, I heard her let out a small gasp.

"Miss . . ." she started to call for Aunt Esther, but for whatever reason she stopped herself. "What did she do to you?" she asked me under her breath as she helped me into the tub. I was thankful she hadn't called for Aunt Esther that morning. I was thankful to have spared her from bearing witness to my scars. Although there were many, they were small and scattered. There was a larger spot on my left thigh, caused by the drippings of boiling water. I like to tell myself that one was an accident.

The water was hot, instantly turning my skin bright red, forcing my eyes to close and my face to wrinkle. Lillian had not noticed. Had she noticed, I am certain she would have drained the tub and began again, filling the tub with cooler, more comfortable water. But, there was a part of me that found pleasure in the scalding. It was as if the water was sterilizing me, stripping away all the layers of grief Mother had caused me through the years. Cleansing me of the mess I had made during the night and of the fit I had caused that morning. The water was washing it all away. Burning it away. In some strange way, I felt as if this were my baptism. This water was making me new.

9

Ida's mother had made us matching dresses. They were for last spring's Easter service. We sat together, in our usual seats, both in pink from head to toe. The dresses were A-lined and there were small white flowers embroidered along the edges. They were beautiful and the ladies in the congregation had complimented her work for weeks after. As I pulled this dress out of my trunk and over my head, I wondered what Ida was doing just then. Pining away for one of the Lansing brothers no doubt. The thought of her daydreaming about these fuzzy - headed boys brought a smile to my face.

"I could tame more than that head of hair," I could hear her saying.

"Sweet Ida," I said aloud, missing her terribly. "I wish you were here," I told her memory.

Aunt Esther had told me to put on my favorite dress. She wanted to try her hand at painting portraits. As I ran my hands down the front of my thighs straightening the skirt, it dawned on me that Ida and I had never had our picture taken together. As I made my way down the hallway, I wished more than ever that Ida was there to share in the joy, and to have her face frozen in time alongside of mine.

"You look sweet enough to eat!" Aunt Esther exclaimed as I entered her studio. "Sit here!" Aunt Esther had prepared a place for me on a large sofa that was covered in pillows. "This could take a while, perhaps more than just today. Are you certain you don't mind being my guinea pig?"

"I'm certain."

"Then let's begin, shall we? Make yourself comfortable."

Doing just as I was told, I leaned into the stack of pillows and squirmed until I found the perfect spot.

"This is going to be so much fun," Aunt Esther kept saying to herself as she stood, mixing her paints and adjusting her easel.

With an apron wrapped around her waist and paintbrush in hand, she stood still as a statue, studying me. At last she approached the canvas, and with a gentle hand, began making small, elegant strokes with her long, slender brush. She would step to one side and quickly glance at me, then return her attention to the canvas. Pretty soon, she began humming to herself. A tune I had heard before.

"My diddy sings that song," I told her, breaking her concentration.

"What's that, Dear?" She asked, poking her head out from behind her easel.

"That song, my diddy sings that."

"Oh." She thought for a moment as if she didn't realize she had been humming at all. "Oh, yes, our mother sang that as she strolled around the house. I suppose it's ingrained in the both of us. A beautiful song, don't you think?"

"I do," I answered, watching a bird glide by the window. It circled around and perched on the windowsill for a brief moment. It looked in at me, then picked up a small piece of something from the ledge and flew away again.

"It doesn't seem right," I said aloud.

"What's that, Dear?"

"It doesn't seem right . . . I'm just sitting here. I should be working. I've never been allowed to just sit and do nothing."

"You aren't doing nothing, you're posing for me. Besides, if you ask me, you were overdue a holiday. So then, no more complaining, just sit and enjoy yourself. I imagine there will be plenty of work for you when you return home." She poked her head out long enough to show me her smile.

When at last Aunt Esther excused me from her studio, I found that Ida was still on my mind. She had been since I put on the dress her mother had made. It was time for me to write the first of what would become a long stream of letters. With pen and paper in hand, I found my way out back, in search of a quiet place to tame the joy I felt before it bubbled over onto the page like childish nonsense. I wanted to share with Ida how Aunt Esther had painted me. How she had removed me from the stack of pillows and had placed me on the earth, under Ol' Willy. How, with her paintbrush, she had unbraided my hair and let it dangle over my shoulders. She had given me my safe haven. A tangible memory of the one place I felt safe. I wanted to share my every emotion with Ida. But, at the same time, I selfishly wanted to keep it to myself.

When Aunt Esther assured me there was a bit of grass in the back, she meant just that. I stepped out of her back door onto a rectangular - shaped patio holding an oval glass - top table surrounded by four metal high-backed chairs. I felt as though I were stepping into an atrium that had fallen victim to high winds causing the roof to blow away. The sides and back of the yard were bricked in. The walls stood well over seven feet tall and were covered in vines and ivy. At the base of each wall stood groupings of green and yellow bushes. There were large stones giving way to rose bushes and every type of flower imaginable. Some were in colorful pots, though most bravely stuck their heads out from the moss - covered ground. They came together leaving a perfect circle in the center of the yard. The bit of grass Aunt Esther had promised me.

All of this, this beauty, could only be seen by my mind's eye. The reality of what lay before me was quite different. We were nearing winter and the ivy was more brown than green, and where the flowers should have been was instead covered in the earth-toned leaves. I could, however, see the garden's potential, thanks to a painting I had seen in Aunt Esther's studio. I did not know at the time she had used her own backyard as the inspiration, but it made sense to me now. I stood in the center of the circle and turned to look up at her studio window. I could picture her standing there with her window open, paintbrush in hand, capturing the essence of the beauty below her to use as a reminder on a day such as this. A reminder that beauty often lives in the memory, not within reach.

I took a seat at the glass-top table, not knowing at the time how many years I would spend sitting there, writing letters. That day, I wrote my first letter to Ida, then went up and visited the studio to soak in all the colors that made up Aunt Esther's painting. Just in case I wasn't there come spring to see it for myself.

Dear Ida,

I am at the end of my first full day here in New York. I miss you already. How is everyone? Tell them all that I am quite well. Lillian is the best cook I have ever known and Aunt Esther is an artist! She began a portrait of me this morning. I am almost embarrassed to say I spent the entire day sitting on feather pillows. Tomorrow, however, will be different. I start my studies at nine in the morning. Aunt Esther has decided to tutor me. She wants to teach me French! I don't expect to ever visit France, but then again, I never expected to visit New York! I don't know what to expect, but I know it would be much more exciting if you were here. I miss you so much, write me soon.

All my love,
Delitha

Dear Delitha,

It was so good to hear from you. I have been worried that you would forget about me. Is New York all you thought it would be? Life here is just as you left it. Momma said your folks are expected back later this week. Does that mean you will be coming home too? I will bake you a batch of cookies when you come. Bring me back something, will you? I may never make it to New York.

We got a letter from Jake, he's living in . . .

"Please put the letter down, Delitha." Aunt Esther stood watching as I folded Ida's letter and stuffed it in my pocket. "You can read your letter a hundred times over, as soon as we are finished here."

I simply smiled at her, appreciative of her efforts. She moved to the front of the room and sat behind her desk. The picture perfect teacher.

"I would like you to open your Reader, beginning on page twelve and going through page twenty-one." She paused and shuffled some papers, "While you are reading I will be preparing a short quiz. Not to worry, though," she winked at me, "everyone passes in my class." She smiled and picked up her pen. "Go on then, read away."

I couldn't tell you what the story was about that day or how well I did on my quiz. The lesson was of little importance, or should I say, it had very little impact on me. What comes to mind when I think of my lessons and of Aunt Esther pretending to be my teacher, is how loved I felt. I remember I would read a few lines and then look up, then read a few more lines, and then look up again. Looking up at this woman that had saved me, this woman who had plucked me from the darkness and placed me into the light. The irreplaceable light of love.

10

My Dearest Del,

I pray this letter finds you happy and in good health. You are missed beyond words. The house seems so quiet without you here. I pray every day that your mother will thrive again and that we can send for you quickly. As for now, the doctors say only time will tell. They can only speculate on the manner of her recovery.

I had hoped to have you home for your birthday. But, there is no celebration here, my love. When I think of the day you left, it never crossed my mind that you would be gone this long. I had such confidence that your mother would improve at the hospital and that by now we would be a family again. What a reminder that life is not always what we think it will be. I do find solace in the knowledge that you are being cared for in a manner that you could not receive here. You are in good hands, Del, and this has given me the peace of mind to give your mother the care she needs. I know you understand.

I have made arrangements with your Aunt Esther for your birthday. Your wish is her command! Enjoy your day; I will be anxious to hear of it.

All my heart to you,
Diddy

It was Monday, the first day of what was sure to be a wonderful week. I woke to the sweet smell of cinnamon rolls, but had trouble moving from my window. The sun was beginning to show its face, allowing the frost to glisten like diamonds. There were bits of ice on my window, arranged around the edges, leaving a perfect oval in the center. From where I stood, it appeared as though the window was a frame and my reflection was the picture inside. I wanted to stand there forever, frozen in time.

"Child, git yourself downstairs." Lillian had let herself in my room. She stood with her hands on her hips, a stained apron around her waist. The smell of cinnamon had followed her through the door.

"You like cold buns?" she asked.

"No ma'am," I answered, my smile growing bigger.

"Then git yourself downstairs and eat' em while they're hot!"

"Yes, ma'am."

I washed my face and dressed as quickly as I could, then started down the stairs. I would never forget how cool the banister felt as I placed my hand on the wood, the tick of the hall clock, or the look in Aunt Esther's eyes when she saw me. We smiled at one another, the kind of smile that stretches your entire face. The kind of smile that almost hurts.

Aunt Esther and Lillian had spent the morning decorating the front room with streamers and balloons. There was a table set by the front window and it was covered with boxes. Boxes of all sizes and wrapped in the prettiest paper I had ever seen. There was a banner draped on the table that read, "Happy Birthday to our Delitha." Never before had such a celebration taken place in my honor. I might as well have just been crowned Miss America. Nothing could have made me feel more special.

"It's all so beautiful," I exclaimed, my eyes filling with tears.

"It's all for you, Dear. Come and enjoy it."

Aunt Esther reached out her hand, and I quickly met her at the bottom step.

"Happy birthday," she said, kissing my cheek.

"Happy birthday," Lillian echoed.

I wrapped one arm around each of them and the three of us stood still and silent, until a buzzer sounded from the kitchen, stealing Lillian from my embrace.

"Come and sit," Aunt Esther whined. "Wipe your eyes before you make me cry as well. I refuse to cry at parties and yours is no exception." She pulled a handkerchief from her pocket and waved it at me. "Come now, take it and let's celebrate."

We stood before the feast of gifts.

"I don't know where to begin," I told her. Never in my life had I been the center of such attention. I couldn't begin to explain what I was feeling. There are words like, loved, fulfilled and complete . . . but they are just words and when you have a feeling as wonderful as this, words are simply not enough. I remember closing my eyes and telling myself that I was luckiest girl in the entire world. It was all so much, not just the gifts but this new life. I simply did not know where to begin.

"Begin here," Lillian called. I turned to find her holding a tray of warm cinnamon rolls, thirteen to be exact, each one holding a pink candle with orange fire dancing about. Aunt Esther took the tray from her and set it on the table.

"Blow them out before the house catches fire," Lillian teased.

"One, two, three! Make a wish!" Aunt Esther yelled, then she burst into a fit of laughter as I blew them out. We each picked up a roll and quickly devoured the sweet, sticky treasure. Despite the napkins Lillian had placed before us, we each sat licking the icing from our fingers.

"Stop the torture," Lillian finally blurted. "Let the poor child open her gifts."

There were so many, I hardly knew where to begin. It was Aunt Esther that finally decided for me. "Open this one," she said, handing me a rectangular box wrapped in pink paper that had been scented like roses.

"It could be anything," I said to myself as I tore the paper. As I lifted the lid, my eyes found a brand new pair of black leather boots.

"You'll need to keep those feet warm. Winter is coming, you know."

"You can try them on later," Lillian said, pulling them from my hands. "This one is from me," she bragged as she replaced the shoes with another box. Inside were hair ribbons of every color imaginable. She simply smiled as I thanked her. Her energy was spent trying to fight the urge to cry. As were we all.

My diddy always said that the giving of a gift is the giving of a heart, putting in place a bond that should never be broken. He was right. We all felt it. They weren't just giving me gifts to celebrate my birthday. They were giving me pieces of their hearts, accepting me into their home, into their lives.

"Here is one that arrived just this morning," Lillian said with a sniffle. "All the way from Georgia."

"From my diddy?" I asked.

She didn't answer. Instead she handed me a small velvet box tied shut with red ribbon. Inside, placed upon a pillow all its own, was a gold chain and locket.

"Open it," Lillian whispered.

The locket opened with a gentle tug; there on its walls were the faces of my parents. To the left my diddy, to the right, Mother. They looked happy, young and vibrant. Not the people I knew that were waiting for me back home. They almost seemed foreign. Parents I had made up, to replace ones I had lost.

"It's beautiful," I said setting the locket back on its pillow. "I'll write to them this evening and tell them how nice it is."

Aunt Esther picked up the necklace and swung it around my neck. After fastening the back, the locket rested on my breastbone.

"Your father gave me specific instructions that you are to wear this at all times," she bent over and spoke in my ear. "He fears you will forget them." She kissed my cheek while she was there, then stood and reached for another gift.

I spent the next half-hour or so being showered with things I had never asked for. Things I needed, such as stockings and slips. Then there were things I never knew I wanted such as scented shampoo and bracelets of different colors. There were a few gifts I might have asked for had I thought of it, such as books, sketch pads, and coloring pencils. Aunt Esther had thought of everything.

"You're not going to believe this," she sang, "but there is one more gift."

"No," I said to her in a solemn voice. "I don't need anything else."

"Ah, well. This is something you do need. Something we should have already taken care. We have an appointment in one hour to get you fitted."

"Fitted?"

"Fitted," she said again. Then, brushing at her midsection she said with a pretend sense of arrogance, "by my personal seamstress."

****

"Here we are," she sang stopping before a shop whose sign read, 'Demsky's'. Aunt Esther had been a faithful customer to the Demsky family business for years, and it intrigued me how excited she was to take me there. It was as if she had been the first to discover a hidden treasure and her joy came from sharing the gold with me.

"Mizz Hancock! Vhat a pleasant surprize," announced a tall, slender man from behind the counter. He wore dark brown slacks with suspenders over an almost white button - down shirt. His sleeves were rolled up to his elbows exposing his forearms, which were covered in curly, graying hair. As he rushed toward us, he began calling the name "Viva." A small woman, whom I assumed was Viva, appeared from behind a hanging curtain.

"Esther," she said, smiling, "How nice to see you." The two women embraced as good friends might do.

"This is my niece, Delitha," Aunt Esther said motioning to me with both hands.

"Vhat a beauty," Viva said, extending her arms to embrace me as well. She was very pretty, plain. She smelled stale and her hair was dry. Her hug was soft and genuine. I liked her immediately.

"Delitha doesn't have suitable clothing for the winter. I was hoping you could whip her wardrobe into shape."

Viva stood back and looked me up and down. Then a smile began growing across her face. "This vill not be verk," she said smiling. "This vill be a treat."

Before I knew it, I was standing before three large mirrors; Viva had instructed me to strip down to my slip while she went to 'gather a few things'. I remember feeling as though I were not alone. I turned and examined the room before I began undoing the long strand of buttons holding my dress together. It was when I hung my dress on the hook that I saw him. Not him, but his eye. There, at my shoulder level was a small hole that should have provided a view of the next room. Instead, it exposed a dark brown, spying eye.

"What are you doing?" I yelped, wrapping my arms around myself.

"I think you're pretty," the voice whispered. Then, before I could respond, the hole was plugged with a small piece of mismatched wood and the eye was gone.

"Knock-knock," Viva called as she slowly opened the door. Her arms were full of sketches and swatches of colored fabric.

"You vill be the envy of all the young ladies ven I am done vith you," her broken accent seemed to tickle my skin.

"You are from Georgia, no?"

"Yes, ma'am."

"I am far from home myself. Been in the states fourteen years now. Our boy vas only two at the time. Your Aunt vas my first customer."

"The very first?" I asked.

"The very first," Viva laughed to herself. "She has changed a lot through the years, no?"

"I don't know," I answered, not knowing what she meant. "I have only known her a short time."

"Ah, I understand. Our families vould not know our boy if they saw him now." She moved around me quickly taking my measurements. "It is very sad how families scatter."

She quickly scribbled on a small pad of paper. "Go and get your Aunt, now. She vill vant to help pick the patterns. Fine taste, that one."

In the lobby I found Aunt Esther sitting before a mirror with a dozen hats scattered about her. She was talking with Viva's husband, Efraim, who was adjusting the hats as she placed them on her head.

"She is such a joy," I heard her say. "I just don't think about the fact that they might send for her tomorrow." I saw her eyes move in the mirror and catch me in the reflection. "Oh, Delitha. That was quick."

"Viva wants your help," I told her.

"Oh my. She doesn't need anyone's help. Give her a needle and thread and a bed of roses and I'd bet she could make a dress of it."

"Ah! You are too kind," Efraim beamed as he gathered the hats.

Viva, Aunt Esther, and I spent the next two hours fretting over the perfect fabric for the perfect style of the perfect dress, for, what Esther saw as, the perfect young lady.

It was almost two weeks later that my new dresses arrived. I had finished my lessons and had retreated to the kitchen for a mid-morning snack.

"Carrot cake," Lillian announced as she slid a piece in front of me, along with a glass of ice cold milk.

"Where did you learn to bake like this?" I asked her as I took my first bite.

"My momma. She could bake anything and everything. Never in my life did she put somethin' on the table that wasn't like eatin' gold."

"You really liked your mother, didn't you?"

"What child don't like their momma?" she asked, handing me a napkin.

I didn't respond.

"No one's momma's gonna be perfect," she said slowly. "They all make mistakes." She patted me on the head as she passed by. "One day, when you're a momma, you'll know what I'm talkin' about."

Then we heard it. A confident rap, tap at the door.

"Why do people refuse to ring the bell?" Lillian huffed. She had just placed her hands in a bowl of raw chicken.

"Run and open it up, will you? If it's for your aunt, have them wait in the parlor. She'll be down shortly."

"Yes, ma'am."

It wasn't for Aunt Esther at all. Behind the door on our top step, stood a very handsome young man. He was dressed in brown pants and a matching vest and overcoat. His hat, which was black, seemed to perfectly match his dark curly hair. On his face was an intoxicating smile and in his hands were long boxes all tied together with string.

"My dresses!" I exclaimed. Then, I blushed for having acted so giddy.

"I can bring them in for you," he said. And he did, marching right into the foyer and placing them on the desk. He walked back to the door and stood there, as if he were waiting for something.

"Thank you," I offered.

He stood still.

"What fun, your dresses have arrived!" Aunt Esther was coming down the stairs, smiling from ear to ear. She walked straight to the desk and opened the side drawer. There was a small wooden box from which she pulled a large coin.

"Here you are then," she said, placing the coin in his outstretched hand.

"Thank you, ma'am. Good day."

"Good day to you." And she turned her attention to me. "Let's get these dresses out and look at them, shall we?" She picked up the boxes and headed for the kitchen. "Lillian is dying to see them."

I took a step or two, following Aunt Esther to the kitchen, when I realized the boy had not moved. He was still standing at the door, waiting. As I turned and walked toward him, I noticed he had pulled the rim of his hat down over his eyes. I'm certain he thought I would not recognize them. These eyes of his . . . eyes the color of the earth. Eyes that sent warmth through my entire body.

"Well, good day then," I said to him with a half smile.

"Good day," he echoed.

I took hold of the door as he walked backwards down the front steps. From under the brim of his hat, he never took his eyes off me. When he reached the bottom step, he reached into his pocket and pulled out a long stick of black licorice. Snapping off a bit with his teeth, he turned to be on his way.

"Wait!" I called to him, stepping down where he could still see me. "I think you're pretty, too."

11

One day, there was a brisk wind flying about the city, shaking signs and scooting objects that were not firmly in their place. The colors of the city were forced to mingle as they were tossed about. The following morning, the entire city was dressed in white. Those who had grown accustomed to the ways of father winter moved about the city as if nothing had changed. I, on the other hand, stood at my window staring at the white intruder terrified by its bulk.

"Beautiful," Lillian said, entering my room.

"I suppose so," I told her under my breath.

She stood behind me, unknowingly pressing her round belly against my back.

"Imagine it's ice cream," she suggested.

"Ice cream?"

"Sure, imagine we had us an ice cream storm. The whole city's been covered up by vanilla."

Her gut moved up and down as she breathed.

"Hmm. That does make it more pleasant," I said, moving as close as I could to the window.

"Good Morning. The snow has arrived!" Aunt Esther announced as she burst into the room wearing her full-length fur coat. "I love it when it snows." She made several big turns showing off her mink.

"I'd love it too, if I had a big animal to keep me warm." Lillian waved Aunt Esther away and started out the door.

"Lillian, we go through this every winter. Let me buy you a new coat." Lillian waved her off again and thumped down the stairs.

"Well," Aunt Esther sighed, turning to me, "I was out and about last week and I picked something up for you." She reached inside her coat, which was buttoned from the bottom and only halfway up. "Tada!" she exclaimed, as though she had pulled a bunny from a top hat.

"It's beautiful!"

"Try it on!"

I twisted and turned until it was just right. Aunt Esther and I stood side by side before my mirror. We stood side by side, with matching smiles, and matching full-length mink coats.

"Take that thing off and give me a hand," Lillian ordered as I entered the kitchen.

"I'm breaking it in," I told her as I rubbed my hands up and down the smooth fur. "It tickles my neck." I said, giggling.

"Alright, fancy pants. Come and help me. We got guests comin' for dinner tonight."

"Tonight?"

"Yup. Your aunt has this ladies club that meets every so often. Once a year they have a fancy dinner. This time she's hostin'."

"Am I invited?" I asked eagerly.

"I suppose so. She'll want to show you off."

She looked at me out of the corner of her eye and tried hard to hide her smile.

Without another word, she picked up my hands and pressed them down into a bowl of bread dough.

"Knead," she said.

Aunt Esther spent the afternoon arranging and rearranging the centerpiece on the dining room table. When she was finally satisfied, she led me to her bedroom with a bowl of chocolates to help pick out her most flattering evening gown.

"Who are these people anyway?" I asked with a mouthful.

"Friends," she answered simply.

"Men? Women?"

"Women."

"Do they have names? How do you know them? Do they have husbands?"

"Delitha . . . does chocolate always make you this excited?"

"No," I told her, feeling silly. "But fancy dinners do."

She stood before her mirror holding an emerald green, sequin dress.

"These ladies are dear friends. We met several years ago in Washington at a rally for . . ." She stopped, turned, and faced me. "You really don't need to know all this, Darling. They are simply friends of mine and I am certain they will all fall deeply in love with you." She approached the bed and stole a chocolate ball from my bowl. "In fact, I bet there will be a fight at the end of the evening over who gets to take you home."

She returned to her wardrobe and pulled out a royal blue dress. It was tight at the waist and trickled down her legs in layers. The bust was sequin and dipped daringly low.

"My favorite necklace and earrings go with this dress," She said to herself in the mirror.

"That's the one, then. It's lovely."

"The problem is," she said, walking over and taking another chocolate ball, "I can't remember what I wore last year. I knew I should have had another one made."

"Well," I offered, "If *you* can't remember, what are the chances anyone else will remember?"

"Good point," she said smiling. "You are such a smart girl. Just like your father." She blew me a kiss. "This is the one. Now, what shall you wear?"

There was no real question to what I was going to wear. Viva had made me a dress for special occasions and this would be the first time I would wear it. It too, was royal blue. There were more ruffles and layers than I knew what to do with.

"You look absolutely beautiful," Aunt Esther gushed as I made my way down the stairs. "Lillian, doesn't she look absolutely beautiful?"

"Pretty as a picture," Lillian agreed dusting flour from her chest and sounding less than impressed. I offered to help Lillian with the last details of the meal. But, she refused my offer for fear of soiling my dress and I found myself sitting alone in the library until at last the doorbell rang.

"Dorothy! How lovely you look! It is so good to see you. Pauline, welcome to my home, you look stunning!" I could hear Aunt Esther's smile even though I couldn't see it.

I peeked around the corner and watched the women file in one by one. Lillian stood by to catch the coats and gloves as they were shed, and once uncovered, each of the ladies sparkled from head to toe. They all looked to be around Aunt Esther's age and equal in her social standing. They all carried themselves with confidence and intelligence. Intimidation overwhelmed me and I closed the door to the library and sat behind Aunt Esther's desk.

I had only been at her desk for a moment, but my curiosity got the best of me and I began opening her desk drawers. The top drawer was filled with stationary and smelled of dried flowers. To the side were two drawers I couldn't wait to get my hands into. Although, after opening the first one, I never made it to the second. For inside the top drawer was a stack of magazines. Magazines were a luxury I had never been given, and I immediately picked up the top copy and began flipping through the pages. The pages were not filled with fashion ideas as I had expected. I closed the magazine and examined the cover.

"Outlook Magazine," I said aloud. "1915."

I began flipping through the pages again until I came to a page bearing a familiar face. Aunt Esther stood on top of a wooden box. She wore a large hat with a feather pointing up to the sky. Her mouth was open, but she was not smiling. She looked angry as she gripped a flag in her raised hand. There was a sash across her chest that read "VOTES for WOMEN." The image frightened me as it revealed a side of her I had never seen. My heart began beating heavily. Her face, the same one that always wore a shine and smile, was twisted and crude. Captured and frozen in time at a moment that transformed her into another being. Someone else's Aunt Esther.

"Child, git yourself in the dining room," Lillian's voice was low but it still startled me. I quickly closed the magazine and shoved it back into the drawer.

"You know better than to go snoopin' in other folk's belongin's."

"Yes, ma'am," I said stumbling out of the room.

Lillian took hold of my arm as I passed by her, my heart still racing.

"Hey," she said, trying for my attention. "I won't tell her you were in her desk, if you won't tell her I dropped one of the chickens on the floor."

She smiled so big I caught sight of a crack in her side tooth.

"Deal," I said smiling back.

"Ah, here she is," Aunt Esther announced, drawing everyone's attention to me. "This is my darling niece, Delitha. Isn't she lovely?"

The ladies offered a collective "ah" and began whispering compliments. I couldn't get to my seat fast enough. I had imagined the evening going much differently. I had pictured myself making a grand entrance into the room and presenting myself as the lady Aunt Esther was preparing me to be. I would greet all the guests one by one, committing each name to memory, and joining them at the table as an equal. That, like I said, was how I had imagined the evening. In all reality, I set foot in the dining room, my heart still racing from the picture I had just found of Aunt Esther. My eyes shot around the room from woman to woman trying to find an explanation for what I had found. The ladies all looked nice enough. They were elegant and proper. They greeted me with kind, warm smiles. They were lovely, just like Aunt Esther. But, my fear was, at any moment, one of them might whip out a sash and flag, stand up on a chair, and begin twisting her face the way Aunt Esther had done. Who were these people?

I went from the door to my seat as quickly as I could and still be considered a lady. Aunt Esther wrapped her arm around me, and as lightly as she could as to not leave a trace of lipstick, she pecked me on the cheek. "I'm so thankful you're here," she said to me. And in that moment, all my fears melted away. I was reminded of the security I felt with her. And I assured myself that whatever caused Aunt Esther to act in such a manner, must have been a worthy cause.

Within moments of my arrival, the ladies forgot I was among them and they began chatting away, sharing secrets and stories that brought smiles and laughter. Lillian circled the table carrying a large bowl of salad, which she began serving to Aunt Esther's guests. I seemed to be the only one in the room that noticed her. She moved around the table like a ghost. Unseen and unheard.

"Pauline, give us a report," one woman spoke up.

Another lady clanked her spoon on her glass, "Attention everyone, attention."

Pauline, who had been placed at the head of the table, stood from her seat, still chewing the first bite of her salad.

"Let me start by saying, how *good* it is to see all of you again. And, congratulations once again for getting the job done!"

"Hear, hear!" The ladies began clapping and cheering aloud, looking at one another and exchanging nods.

"It's been a long, hard battle, ladies."

"But we won!" Aunt Esther interrupted.

"Amen!" another lady spoke up.

"Hear, hear!" the ladies chattered again.

"We are here tonight to remember the fight and celebrate the victory.

Drink up!"

And with that, all the ladies picked up their wine goblets and pressed them into the center of the table.

"Cheers!" they sang in unison. And as if directed by a conductor, they pressed the goblets to their lips and drank.

Pauline cleared her throat and set her goblet back in its place.

"Let's all thank our top orator for opening her home. Thank you, Esther."

"Yes, thank you," the ladies offered.

"Now, let's stop our gabbing and eat!" Pauline demanded.

The ladies offered a round of applause once more and then began mumbling to one another as they picked at their salads.

I had been placed between Aunt Esther and a lady that still smelled damp from the winter storm that raged just outside our front door. Her skin was pale and looked extraordinarily thin.

"You look very pretty this evening," she said to me.

"Thank you. You look very pretty too," I told her. Then I pinched myself on the leg for not offering a more dignified response.

"Your name is Delitha?"

"Yes, ma'am."

"My name is Elizabeth."

"It's very nice to meet you," I said, rubbing the sting away from my self - inflicted pinch.

"Are you enjoying your stay here, with your aunt?"

"Very much, thank you."

"You know, your Aunt Esther is a very special woman. She changed the world, she did."

"We all did," Aunt Esther said, leaning in and winking at me.

"Pauline, how was Washington?" asked the lady sitting across from Aunt Esther.

Elizabeth leaned in to me but spoke loudly enough for everyone to hear, "Pauline had the privilege of meeting Mrs. Roosevelt."

Before I could respond, Aunt Esther was tugging at my seat.

"Delitha, I am so very sorry. I don't know what I was thinking. You need to concentrate on being a child. There will be plenty of time for you to worry yourself with adult . . ."

85

"Oh let her listen in," Pauline interrupted. "She needs to know why she'll never play bugle for a suffragist band. Or, rather, why she'll never *have* to."

When I heard the word "suffragist" it all made sense to me. I remember feeling as though I were being handed a right of passage from childhood into womanhood. Mother had read the papers once and had voiced that she was suffering enough. That she would have no part of this movement toward women's rights. I was seeing more and more the gap between Mother and my Aunt Esther. I was beginning to see pieces of myself in each of them. I had no desire to stand on a soapbox and voice my opinion to the crowd below. Yet, sitting with those women made me feel empowered. Made me feel important. Made me feel alive.

"You want to stay, don't you child?" Pauline asked leaning over the table.

"Very much," I answered.

Aunt Esther glared down at me with squinted eyes.

"Oh, very well," she finally sang.

"Oh wonderful!" one woman said aloud. The other ladies raised a fist in agreement.

Pauline took her seat and wiggled around for a moment finding the most comfortable spot. Then, pressing at her hair she began her story.

"Mrs. Roosevelt . . . well, where should I begin?"

The ladies sat on the edges of their seats with great anticipation. All the ladies, except for Aunt Esther and Elizabeth; they both set to work on their salads.

"You know," Elizabeth whispered, leaning in to me. "Your Aunt Esther was the first to be chosen."

"Chosen?"

"Chosen to go to Washington. Esther was first in line to chat with Mrs. Roosevelt."

"What happened? Why didn't she go?" I asked, louder than I had meant to.

"Oh, Liza stop it!" Aunt Esther scolded under her breath. She then picked up my fork and placed it in my hand.

I picked through the greens, paying no attention to Pauline and her description of the first lady. My mind was racing. What on earth could have been more important than meeting the First Lady? What could have kept her from going to Washington?

I had just taken my first bite when I felt Elizabeth's lips press against my ear. A shiver trickled down my spine as she spoke.

"She didn't go to Washington to meet Mrs. Roosevelt because she went to meet someone more important in Georgia."

12

Del,

I am writing you by candlelight. It is well into the night but I cannot sleep. Your mother is restless and nothing can calm her. I had hoped to inform you that her condition had improved. However, that is not the case. She seems to be growing weaker, more distant. I do not wish to frighten you, but I feel you are able to grasp the truth. You will need to stay with Esther a while longer. My only comfort is the word I receive from her, Esther says you are happy. That you are laughing, and glowing as a young lady should. I am forever in debt to her for bringing you back to life.

All my love,
Diddy

In one of his many letters, my diddy said that I was coming back to life. I read those words over and over. The word "back" kept grabbing my attention. I didn't feel as though I were coming "back" to life. I felt as though I had, for the very first time, been given life. My voice was stronger, my laugh louder. My smile was wider, and a new shade of rosy pink had covered my skin. I felt strong and smart. I began holding my head up as I walked and my feet seemed to carry me with a confidence that had been hiding within me. I was happy. I was new.

New. A word we used quite often during my first year with Aunt Esther. She continued to teach me, not only book lessons but life lessons as well. Though the snow had mostly melted, and spring was just around the corner, it was still too cold for my liking.

"It's freezing," I complained as Carlton opened the car door for me.

"It is rather chilly today, isn't it?" Aunt Esther tugged on her gloves as she wiggled to get comfortable in her seat. "Trust me; you'll have forgotten all about this chill once you see where we're going. You do like the carnival don't you?" She raised her eyebrows.

"I've never been to the carnival," I confessed, feeling my aggravation turning to anticipation.

"You've never been to the carnival? Carlton, have you ever heard of such nonsense . . . a child having never been to the carnival?"

"A cryin' shame, ma'am," Carlton answered with the most monotone of voices.

"A crying shame indeed!" Aunt Esther exclaimed. "Never been to the carnival. Hmph. Well, then today shall be even more special than I had expected." She smiled at me and cocked her head. "Never been to the carnival" she said again patting my leg. "I am so pleased to be the first to take you."

One of my favorite things was riding in Aunt Esther's car. I loved watching the city move past my window. The city was constantly changing. There were new sites to be seen each and every time we went out.

"Shall I wait for you ma'am?" Carlton asked.

"What a marvelous question," Aunt Esther sang teasingly.

"A marvelous question indeed," I chimed in.

"Ma'am?" Carlton asked again after clearing his throat.

"Are we here? Already?" My heart was racing as I peered out the window and spotted a sign reading 'Central Park'.

"Central Park? We've been to Central Park." A pang of disappointment swept over me.

"You've never been to Central Park on a day like today," Aunt Esther assured me, stepping from the car.

"Ma'am? Shall I wait for you?" Carlton asked again, seeming the slightest bit annoyed.

"Now, Carlton," Aunt Esther snapped, placing her hand on his arm. "You have been my driver now for what . . . twelve years? Please stop calling me ma'am." She removed her hand from his arm and gestured to me, "What is my name?"

"Esther," I answered proudly. After all, it was the most beautiful name I had ever heard.

"Esther," she repeated. "My name is Esther. And no, there is no need to wait for us. I would say by . . . oh, four o'clock we should be ready to return home. Will that work alright with your schedule?"

We all stood in silence for a moment.

"Have a good day, miss," Carlton said to me. "Ma'am," he said to Aunt Esther, tipping his hat. As the car pulled away, Aunt Esther simply smiled and shook her head, saying, "That man. . ."

We passed the stone entrance with a crowd of smiling people. Aunt Esther was right, the chill in the air seemed to disappear and a feeling of warmth came over us as the carnival came into view. Right inside the gates there were games set up to test a man's strength and wit. There were racks of silly prizes waiting to be claimed by the strongest and smartest of the bunch. Despite the cold, there were men in every line rolling up their shirtsleeves while flexing their forearms for the ladies standing nearby. I couldn't help but laugh out loud. To my surprise, one man heard me and flexed both arms while winking at Aunt Esther and me.

"Never trust a man who shows off his muscles," Aunt Esther said, steering me in the opposite direction. "If a man has to brag about the strength in his arms, it means he can't brag about the strength in his head." She took in a deep breath. "Look at those!" she exclaimed. "Tell me that isn't the most delicious cake you've ever laid your eyes on!" She was pointing to a four - layered white cake with strawberry icing. "Don't tell Lillian, of course, but, that is the most beautiful cake I have ever seen."

It was all beautiful to me. Every inch of the park, every person, every game, every food stand. It was absolutely beautiful.

"What shall we do first?" Aunt Esther said, stopping for a moment. "Take a good look around. We can do it all," she said mischievously. "But, what shall we do first?"

Aunt Esther had followed me back to the front gates. Back to one of the first games we had passed on our way in. We were standing before a long shelf where targets shaped as different animals would stand up giving the player a second's chance to shoot and knock them down again. I had my pellet gun in hand patiently waiting for Aunt Esther to give the two cents needed to play the game. The man behind the counter wore all black and his beard drooped to the middle of his chest. When he saw the coins emerge from Aunt Esther's bag, he showed his toothless grin.

"I'm not sure about this, Delitha. This seems terribly dangerous."

"I didn't think you found anything dangerous," I told her bluntly.

She stood, uncertain of what her response should be.

"I've shot a pellet gun before," I lied. "Ida's brothers would take us hunting."

"Hunting?"

"Sure."

"What on earth did you hunt for?"

"Oh, rabbit," I lied again, this time sounding more confident.

"You hunted for rabbit with a pellet gun?"

"Ladies, there's a line formin'. Are ya in or out?"

"Excuse me?" Aunt Esther turned to see just how many people were behind us.

"We're in," I answered for her, taking the coins from her hand and placing them on the counter.

My Aunt Esther simply leaned against the counter and crossed her arms.

"All right, little miss. Shoot me a rabbit."

Ping. Ping. Ping, went the pellet against the metal targets.

Clank. Clank. Clank, went the targets as they fell backwards.

"Delitha! I don't know what to say," Aunt Esther said, seeming flustered.

"Aha! A natural," said the toothless man. "Don't see too many of them in a skirt."

"I beg your pardon?" Aunt Esther hissed. "Give me that," she said, taking the gun from my hands and handing over another two cents.

"Come on, lady. Let's not get upset," said the man.

"Upset? Whose upset?" Aunt Esther held the gun up and closed her left eye to focus.

"Watch out, old man!" cried a man from behind us. "Don't stand too close to the targets."

Suddenly there was a chorus of manly laughter ringing out behind us.

Although I couldn't help but blush, Aunt Esther never skipped a beat.

Ping. Ping. Ping.

Clank. Clank. Clank.

Suddenly the laughter stopped.

"Aha! We have ourselves two naturals! Congratulations, ladies!"

Aunt Esther handed over the pellet gun and nodded to me with great satisfaction.

The man behind the counter let out a loud belly laugh. "Like mother like daughter, eh?"

Suddenly the world stopped. The carnival disappeared and the only people left on the earth were Aunt Esther, myself, and this man who had just assumed us mother and daughter. For a moment, I felt as though I were being complimented for my trickery. I had pretended so many times to myself that Aunt Esther was in fact my mother, that I had actually fooled someone else into believing my deepest desire. Then, my heart stopped for fear of her correcting him. What would he think of me? He would certainly think me a silly fool for acting in such a manner. Esther was my aunt. Not just any aunt, but an aunt that I had only known for a short time, and I had already, in my mind's eye, put her in the place of my mother. I was no silly fool. I was every mother's worst nightmare. The child that wanted to forget and replace the one that had labored to give her life.

"Well, don't just stand there laughing!" Aunt Esther scolded him. "What have we won?"

"Anything you see here!" the man answered, still laughing. "Pick your fancy."

"All these prizes are for men," Aunt Esther said, surveying the shelf.

"What did you expect?" the man asked, now laughing even harder. "I'll tell you what . . . my wife has a cake stand a row over. Tell her Al sent you. One whole cake for the both of ya."

Aunt Esther looked down at me and squinted.

"I would have preferred something more dignified," she said, holding her chin up. "But, my daughter loves cake. It's a deal."

We walked away hand in hand. My heart was still beating unsteadily.

"You called me your daughter," I managed to say, almost hoping she would not hear me.

"Yes, well, we both told a little white lie now didn't we?"

"What?"

"Delitha, you are a good shot. But, I don't believe for a moment that you went shooting for rabbits with Ida and her brothers."

All I could do was laugh. I laughed extra hard with hopes of pushing the guilt from my gut, up my throat, and out of my mouth, into the open where it could float away and haunt someone else.

****

"This cake is divine!" I managed to say between bites.

Aunt Esther and I had settled for two extremely large pieces of cake rather than two entire cakes that would cause Lillian to doubt her position as our prized baker.

"Divine indeed!" Aunt Esther agreed. "How on earth can someone trap so much flavor in something as simple as a cake? I know a good many things, but the art of cake making and flavor trapping is beyond me!"

We both let out a steady laugh trying hard not to lose one single crumb from our plates. We walked slowly, savoring each and every bite of the strawberry frosting that seemed to double in size the moment it touched the tongue.

"What are they doing?" I asked Aunt Esther pointing to a large group of middle-aged men and women. They were all dressed in long black cloaks and were standing in a circle holding hands.

"They'll be dancing soon," she answered, taking her eyes off her cake for only an instant.

"Dancing?"

Before she could explain, the music began. It was slow to start and the dancers simply began swaying back and forth. Then, as the pace quickened, the men began kicking up their legs as the women turned round and round holding their hands high above their heads.

"How strange," I said to no one in particular.

The music was nothing I had ever heard. Its beat was harsh and dark yet it seemed to invigorate all who were listening. I found it impossible to contain my smile as the dancers once again joined hands and began skipping to the center of the circle. When they stepped back again, there was a young man standing in the center as if someone had simply pulled him from a pocket and set him down.

As they began to dance around, the crowd began to cheer and clap. The dancers began singing with the music.

"I can't understand them."

"What's that dear?" Aunt Esther bent over and pressed her cheek against mine.

"I can't understand them. What are they singing?"

"Ah . . . it's not English. These folks are from . . ." Before she finished her sentence she began laughing out loud. "Do you know who that is, Delitha? I can hardly believe my eyes!" She stood up straight and raised her eyebrows.

"Who is it? What?"

Aunt Esther continued laughing to herself, unable to take her eyes off the young man. It wasn't until the music ended and the applause died down did she answer me.

"That was Yosef!"

"Who?"

"Yosef. The boy that was dancing. That was Viva's boy."

"Viva?"

Then I recognized him.

"Bravo!" Aunt Esther called out to him. He waved back to her and when his eyes caught mine, he stopped. I stood motionless, lost in his gaze. Without taking his eyes off me, he moved his hand to his lips and blew me a kiss. An instant later, the music began again and he spun around like a windstorm starting his next performance.

I was smitten. And like Aunt Esther, I could no longer hide my enjoyment. My laughter rang out above the rest of the crowd, and as I threw my hands together to cheer him on, my plate holding the last precious bites of my strawberry cake, fell to the ground.

13

"He must have danced for two hours! I've never seen anything like it!"

"Yes, so you said. Now in the bath you go."

"I wish you could have been there," I told Lillian, as I stepped into the steaming water. The hair on my legs stood on end and a shiver shot up my spine.

"What on earth would I have done at a carnival?" she replied, placing a hanger on the dress I had just stepped out of. "What is this? Is this frosting on your dress?"

I froze, crouching in the tub, half of me submerged in stinging hot water, half of me exposed to stinging cold air.

"This looks like strawberry frosting." She glared at me with her piercing eyes.

Aunt Esther was coming from her room and overheard Lillian's comment. She began waving her hands and shaking her head behind Lillian's back.

"No," I said, still shivering. "I really don't think that's strawberry frosting."

"It is," she demanded. "I know strawberry frosting when I see strawberry frosting."

I glanced over her shoulder to Aunt Esther, desperately needing to be rescued.

"Lillian . . . have you seen my pearl earrings?"

"What?" Lillian turned to face Aunt Esther. "For heaven's sake, don't tell me you've lost those new pearl earrings?"

"I'm so sorry Lillian . . ."

"Look at this," Lillian interrupted. "Does this look like strawberry frosting to you?"

Without hesitation, Aunt Esther did what she did best, saved the day.

"Why, yes. I do believe that is strawberry frosting." She turned her attention to me. "Delitha, do you know how that got on your dress? Do you remember Miss Sinclair? You remember that lanky woman that wouldn't stop hugging you? Remember she was eating an enormous slice of strawberry cake and I bet you anything she slopped that on your dress." She smiled her sparkling smile. "Lillian I do apologize for her clumsiness. And, Delitha, I am terribly sorry she dirtied your dress. Lillian, dear, do you think you could work your magic and remove this horrid pink frosting before a stain sets in? I do love our Delitha in this dress. I would be so terribly sad if this dress were ruined."

We all stood silent for a moment, awaiting Lillian's reaction. Finally it came.

"Why . . . this is nothin'. I'll have this out in no time." She marched proudly from the washroom, and as she took the first step to the downstairs we heard her say, "I'll work my magic."

Aunt Esther pressed her forefinger to her lips and winked at me with her deceiving eye. I slid the rest of my body down into the liquid paradise and began my nightly ritual of childish daydreaming that in my old life had been forbidden.

Delitha,

Momma made us matching dresses to start the spring season. They are yellow with tiny brown flowers. She made matching handbags as well. I told Momma I wouldn't wear mine until you came home. But, Momma gave it to your father and he said he would mail it to your Aunt Esther's house. I miss you terribly. I love getting your letters. I dream that I am with you, walking the streets of New York licking stacked ice cream cones without a care in the world.

I love you, my friend.
Ida

Ida was always one for good ideas. After reading her letter, I begged Lillian to visit the Marble Bar and Ice Cream Parlor on West 17th. I had already devoured the top scoop when I looked down and saw that a sticky chocolate dollop had landed on the toe of my left shoe.

"How undignified," I whispered, impersonating Aunt Esther. Just as I bent over to wipe my shoe clean, an unexpected voice came from behind me.

"Every time I see you, you're eating."

Startled, I stood up straight. Instinctively, my body swung around in search of the sound that had sent my heart into a fit.

"I beg your pardon," I said, trying my best to seem ladylike.

"I like a girl with a healthy appetite," he chuckled. Then, laying his hand on his chest he simply said, "Yosef." Unlike his parents, this was the only word he spoke with a traceable accent.

"I know your name," I managed to say without blushing.

His smile, along with his ego, seemed to double in size.

"Are you going to share your treat or what?" he finally asked.

"Oh, certainly." I held out my melting chocolate blob, and as he wrapped his fingers around the cone, I hesitated before pulling my fingers out from under his. After taking a long lick, he wiped at his mouth with his shirtsleeve and said, "I'm on my way to rehearsal, wanna come?"

"Rehearsal? For what"

"For what?" He took a step back and shook his head in disbelief.

"Rehearsal for . . . well, let me ask you this. What's one thing you know I can do really well?"

I thought for a moment.

"Peep through tiny holes in the wall…oh wait, you aren't very good at that. I did catch you after all." I felt my heart flutter as I noticed his cheeks turning the slightest shade of pink. "You have dance rehearsal," I told him.

"Well, do you wanna come?" he asked, shuffling his feet. "Everyone there will be famous one day, including yours truly."

Shrugging my shoulders, acting as though I had nothing better to do with my time, I linked my arm through his and breathlessly said, "Oh, why not."

The dance studio was one large room that had been divided into four equal parts by painting bright red lines on the floor. In the far left corner, a dozen little girls in short, white silky skirts and white stockings pranced around attempting to balance on their toes. In the front corner, directly in front of the children, were girls my age and older. They, too, were dressed in silky white, but nothing about them resembled the young girls in back. These young ladies looked like swans as they stretched their bodies and moved effortlessly. In the far right corner were young men dressed in dark baggy pants. They wore no shirts and I felt my eyes go straight to the floor the instant I realized I was looking at bare flesh.

"You can watch from over there," Yosef said, pointing to the front right corner. There were twenty or so chairs lined up against the wall. Two seats were occupied by giggling girls. I took the seat farthest from them and focused my attention on the floor. It was black and dusty. Tiny bits of fuzz flew around with the motion of my feet. "If I had a broom," I said to the floor, "I would sweep you."

There was no music. Each group of dancers would simply mimic their instructor. For the young girls, it was a petite lady in her early twenties. She danced in her own world unconcerned that her students were not following her lead. The older girls were led by a woman wearing black from head to toe allowing her gray hair to shimmer under the lights. I glanced, for only a moment, at the men's instructor. My eyes only made it to his shoulders before I blushed and turned away.

I decided to watch the ladies' instructor. She was strikingly beautiful and there was an air about her that brought Aunt Esther to mind. In my mind, I was picking a tune that was suitable to their movements, when suddenly, I was startled by a flying object that landed at my feet. As I bent over to pick it up, I felt my skin tingle. It was Yosef's shirt.

"Delitha," Yosef was whispering my name, desperately trying for my attention. I tried my hardest not to lift my head. I was mortified at the sight of these men with their chests exposed for all to see.

"Delitha."

I looked up. Then down again.

"Delitha."

I looked up, squinting so that they all looked gray and blurry.

"I brought you here to watch," he said in a louder voice.

Slowly my eyes opened to their normal size. My throat felt tight and my head fuzzy. I blinked and then my fear was realized. Once I laid my eyes on him, I couldn't take them off.

****

"You can come watch anytime you want," Yosef told me.

He had walked me home and we stood facing one another on the top step. His forehead was still red and damp with sweat. We stood, both of us clasping our own hands behind our backs.

"You really are talented," I told him, trying my best to sound flirtatious and not silly.

"Would you like to share some ice cream again tomorrow? My last delivery should be around three."

"Yes," I whispered, pretending he had just asked me to be his wife.

Then, unexpectedly, he leaned in and quickly pecked me on the lips. Before I could give in to my girlhood fantasy of closing my eyes, tilting my head, and raising one foot off the ground ever so slightly, Yosef was down the steps and on his way.

"Tomorrow," he called over his shoulder.

With flushed skin and a pounding heart, I raced through the door and up the stairs to my room. Although this was a letter I would never send, I wrote,

Dear Ida,

I just had my first kiss . . .

14

Everyone has a magical season in their life, even if it is short lived. A season in which the brain captures the smallest of notions and holds onto them as if they were of the utmost importance. That next morning was the beginning of my magical season. I vividly remember the way my pillow felt against my face as I opened my eyes. There was nothing spectacular about the feeling; I had just simply noticed the sensation of the fabric against my skin. The way I had noticed how the coins felt cold as Lillian placed them in the warmth of my palm. And how the breeze gently disturbed my hair the very instant Yosef came into view.

"Good day," he said cheerfully.

I responded with a girlish grin.

"I know you didn't walk all this way just to smile at me, did you?"

"I beg your par . . ."

"I'm just yankin' your cord. Let's get some ice cream."

A small bell jingled against the door as it swung open. I could smell the frost that surrounded the jugs of ice cream.

"Good day, Mr. Matthews." Yosef politely nodded as we stepped inside.

"Good day to you, son." Mr. Matthews straightened his hat and patted his white apron. "The usual?" He asked, smiling down on Yosef.

"Yes, sir."

"Right away, son."

"The usual?" I whispered.

"Sure." Yosef whispered back. "Mrs. Matthews buys all her dresses from my mother. As long as Mrs. Matthews is happy, Mr. Matthews treats me to a scoop of ice cream."

"Here you are." Mr. Matthews bellowed from behind the counter. "Is she with you?" He asked. "Any friend of yours is a friend of mine." Mr. Matthews' smile seemed to grow with every passing moment.

"Yes, sir. She's with me. This is my girl."

"Woa, slow down. Aren't you a bit too young for that?"

"No, sir. I'm only two years away from the age of my parents when they got hitched."

Hitched. The word echoed in my head. I told myself that in two short years Yosef and I would be married. Married! A smile began forming on my face when I heard,

"Woa, let's slow down now. Let's not get ahead of ourselves."

Mr. Matthews smiled at Yosef and Yosef smiled back, both of them seemingly forgetting that I was even in the room. But, I didn't mind. As far as I was concerned, the world was in perfect harmony.

"If I knew I could get free ice cream, I would be here every single day."

"There's no time," Yosef replied. "Between deliveries and rehearsal . . . I'm lucky to get here once a week."

"Once a week!" I exclaimed. "I'd gladly take a free ice cream cone once a week."

"Tell me your cook doesn't make ice cream all the time." He wrinkled his brow when he said this, and I wasn't certain how to respond.

"Well . . . yes, she does. But, it is an entirely different experience getting ice cream in one's own kitchen as opposed to going to an ice cream parlor."

He thought for a moment, taking another large bite from his scoop.

"Doesn't that hurt your teeth?" I asked, but he ignored my question.

"I'm not sure I agree with you. I think it would be great fun to get ice cream in your own kitchen. How about this. Let's eat this ice cream, then we'll go to your Aunt's house and have ice cream there, too. See which we like better."

This time it was me that stopped for a moment to think.

"Lillian would never allow it." I told him.

"She wouldn't have to know," He chuckled. "This was free wasn't it? I bet she gave you money, didn't she?" I didn't answer. "Give her back her money and tell her we wanted *her* ice cream instead. She'll never know."

"I can't lie to Lillian," I told him. "She would know."

"It's not a lie," he assured me. "You do want her ice cream, right?"

I shook my head. "This doesn't sound good. Lillian can read me like a book."

"Then leave it to me," he said proudly.

Before I knew it, we were standing on Aunt Esther's top step.

"I don't like this," I told him. He leaned against the door and watched me take the last few bites of my cone. I wiped at my mouth and brushed off my dress.

"Lillian?" I had called her name six times from the front door to the kitchen and she still had not answered.

"Where is she?" Yosef asked. He was right on my heels and hunched over as if we were trespassing.

"Where's who?" came Lillian's voice from behind the pantry door. She gingerly poked her head out and smiled at us. "Who's your friend?" And before I could answer, Lillian added, "Oh, I know you. You deliver Miss Esther's dresses. You're Viva's boy."

"We were hoping for some ice cream," I said.

"Now hold on a minute." Lillian waddled from the pantry with an arm's load of potatoes. "I thought I gave you ice cream money this mornin'."

Without a word, I held out my hand and presented her with the coins.

Yosef spoke up, "We decided your ice cream was better than what they serve at the parlor."

"We? I don't recall ever servin' you my famous ice cream before."

"Delitha's told me so much about it, I feel like I've already had some." He winked at her. "I know it's the best."

Yosef and I sat across from one another at the table. Lillian served us each a scoop of vanilla bean and gave us free reign with the chocolate topping. The scene had played out much better than I had imagined. I had not needed to lie to Lillian. I had not needed to stretch the truth even the tiniest bit. I looked over at Yosef as he devoured his treat and wondering what he was thinking. Was he as taken with me as I was with him? He had, after all, kissed me on the lips just the night before. Had he not hinted at a proposal in the ice cream parlor? It wasn't until I escorted Yosef to the front door that my heart was put at ease.

"You can't be leaving so soon, I haven't even had a chance to say hello!"

Yosef and I were standing at the door when Aunt Esther appeared at the top of the stairs wearing her painter's smock. Perhaps it was only the light, but from where she stood, she seemed to be radiating. Almost glowing.

"How are you, Yosef? I was so hoping the two of you would meet and strike up a friendship."

"We did, ma'am."

Aunt Esther skipped down the stairs as if she were coming to greet a long lost friend. "I am so pleased," she said smiling. "You know, Yosef, you are always welcome here."

"Thank you, ma'am."

For a reason I cannot explain, my cheeks suddenly felt hot.

Placing her hand on my forehead, Aunt Esther asked, "Delitha, dear, are you feeling alright? You're as red as a beet."

"I'm fine," I said, dying inside of embarrassment.

"I'm the one who should be feeling ill," Yosef said proudly to Aunt Esther.

"Oh, and why is that?" she replied.

"Delitha stole my heart. I should be dead by now."

There was not a sound in the room. Perhaps the entire world had fallen still. The silence was deafening. I desperately needed to say something, to respond to this incredibly romantic moment. Yet, I was frozen. I was paralyzed. All I could do was wait to be rescued from this awesomely awkward moment. It was Lillian that came to my rescue. Lillian and her famous apple pie.

"Take this home with you; give your momma our regards."

Yosef's eyes widened. "Thank you, thank you very much."

"You are very welcome." Lillian patted her apron and headed back to the kitchen. Speaking over her shoulder, she added, "Don't mean to be rude, but I got meals to think about."

"Thank you, Lillian," we all three said only seconds apart from one another.

"It was wonderful to see you, Yosef," Aunt Esther added, opening the door for him. "And Yosef . . . you're heart could not have made a better choice than to be captured by this one." She rested her hands on my shoulders sending a warm rush of energy through my body. Yosef walked backward down the front steps and winked at me before turning to walk away. The door closed, sending Yosef out into the open world and locking me inside.

"Well, that was the sweetest thing I have ever seen!" Aunt Esther exclaimed, turning me to face her. "Now, what have you to say for yourself? Has he stolen your heart too?"

The heat in my face shot up a few degrees.

"Aha!" she exclaimed. "He has! This is so sweet!" She bent down and got close to my face. "We mustn't tell your father. No writing about this in your letters, you hear me? He'd send for you in a heartbeat if he knew I was letting you dabble in love!"

I couldn't help but smile at her enthusiasm. She laughed out loud as she straightened up and took my hand. "Puppy love is so spectacular. Much better than the real thing. You can get over many a loves, but the first one . . . the first one burrows a place in your heart that remains with you all the days of your life."

"Love?" Lillian shouted from the kitchen.

Aunt Esther leaned down and whispered to me, "Oh don't listen to a word she has to say on the subject. Her heart has been tainted."

Before Aunt Esther could finish her sentence, Lillian was coming toward us.

"I would like to think you could use the word 'love' on someone more respectable."

"Lillian don't be silly. Yosef is a fine young man." Aunt Esther stood proudly and spoke as if she had raised the young man herself.

"Child, that boy's mind is on one thang . . . himself." She began shaking her finger at me as she spoke. "You wanna give your heart to a liar, be my guest. But don't say I didn't warn you."

Aunt Esther pulled me toward her as if to protect me from Lillian's flailing finger, "Good heaven's, Lillian, what on earth are you talking about?"

Lillian took one step closer to me and opened her eyes wide.

"I can smell Mr. Matthews' ice cream from a mile away. You let him convince you to lie about somethin' as silly as ice cream . . . well, Lord only knows what else he'll get you to do."

"Delitha?" Aunt Esther turned me around and held me at arm's length.

"I didn't mean any harm," is all I could muster.

"He's not for you," Lillian said turning back to the kitchen. "His parents may be good folk, but that boy is trouble."

Aunt Esther took my hand and began leading me up the stairs. As we walked, she spoke just loud enough for me to hear.

"Only you can choose who you will give your heart to." She looked down at me briefly, then she began giggling at the thought. "Yosef Demsky has stolen your heart."

I laughed along with her as she led me up the stairs. But, I remember thinking, wondering what Mother would have to say. The word nonsense came to mind. I felt myself flinch at her memory and I drove it away with thoughts of Aunt Esther, the one who had really stolen my heart.

15

My letters to Ida seemed to become more and more impersonal, which surprised me because in my heart, I missed her terribly. Yet, day by day, I felt a bit more disconnected from her and from home. I confessed to Ida once that I was losing myself. Every day I felt a piece of myself break off and blow away with the breeze. And it wasn't long before I was no longer losing myself, but I was completely lost. Every piece of my original self was gone. She never responded to my confession, and her absence in my growth changed our friendship.

I had chosen not to tell Ida about Yosef. She knew nothing of his existence. I had written her once with the news of our first kiss, but I tore it in half and tossed it in the trash rather than placing it with the outgoing mail. I had feared she would feel as though she were being replaced. And, perhaps she was. I had chosen not to tell Yosef about Ida because when I was with him, she scarcely entered my mind. Not just Ida, but home. Georgia, my diddy, Mother, Ida. It all seemed like a dream. A dream from my childhood. One that had passed through my mind in a deep sleep. One that left only traces of existence in my memory. One that I could bring forth if I chose to do so. But, I rarely did.

Thoughts of home came only in my dreams, not during the waking hours with the streets of New York calling my name. My name. My name was no longer a series of words that caused me to cringe. New York whispered my name as if we were having a love affair. I was one. An individual. Not a figure that in Mother's mind transformed into five servants. New York respected me and I it. Yes, my letters to Ida were becoming few and far between, but it only takes one letter, one piece of news to change the course of your life.

Delitha,

You're never going to believe this . . . but, we're moving. And not just anywhere but next door to your parents! Daddy says living in town will give Albert more opportunities. I wonder if he ever considered how this might affect me. What will I do in town without you?

Ida

Ida,

I don't know what to say about your move. Why is it that I am here and you are now living directly next door to my parents? This makes no sense to me. I thought Albert wanted to farm like the rest of your family. I admit, my thoughts are everywhere. My heart is aching, and suddenly I feel lost. Or rather, left out.

One thing you can do is check on Ol' Willy for me. How is my silly old tree? Do you suppose he misses me? Silly, isn't it? To think that a tree would miss having a little girl cuddling under its branches. But, why not? Why shouldn't Ol' Willy miss doing what he was intended to do? Visit him, will you?

Write when you are settled in and let me know every detail.

Delitha

Ida's letter came as a surprise. She was now living in the estate next to my parents. Winston Manor had become the home of what was left of the Sunday family. It made no sense to me. Ida's father had been a farmer all his life. It was out of character for him to move into town. He was turning his back on the only life he knew. I wondered how he would make a living there, but I dared not ask. The matters of the family, my diddy would say, are left up to the father . . . and his decisions are not to be questioned.

Del,

Your mother spoke of you in her sleep last evening. She spoke of you as a woman, not a child. My heart grieves knowing you are growing up and we are missing it.

Happy birthday, darling. I have made arrangements with Esther. She will deliver my gift for you as usual. Please do not feel badly toward me. I fear I will never outgrow this guilt I feel.

Diddy

Diddy,

Guilt? You should not associate with the word. I have only spoken briefly of my life here for fear of hurting you. But, if it will set your heart at ease, I will share with you. I am so happy here. I thank the Good Lord everyday you allowed me to come here. Aunt Esther is a wonderful example, she has taught me so much. When I look in the mirror, there is a young lady staring back at me. My fear is that you will not know me when I return.

I have nothing but love for you,

Del

It seemed as though Mother and I were living by two different timelines. Mother's condition was slowly worsening. Yet, my life seemed to be moving forward as quickly as the train that delivered me here. One day I was looking in the mirror at a weary child, the next day I was looking at a radiant young lady.

"Where have the years gone?" Lillian asked as she set the traditional pan of cinnamon rolls before me. "You've turned into a fine young lady. A fine young lady, indeed."

"Hush now," Aunt Esther ordered. "Let her blow out the candles . . . and don't forget to make a wish," she said, clapping her hands together. I loved how her excitement never failed. I had told her once that it would be gift enough to wrap up her energy and place a bow on top.

After breakfast we made our usual trip to see Viva and fit me with a new, prizewinning wardrobe. Or so I thought. To my surprise when we entered the shop, there was no one to be found.

"Perhaps they're in the back room," Aunt Esther hinted, pretending to be annoyed. She tapped on the door leading to the changing rooms, and we heard a familiar voice say, "Do come in."

Efraim, Viva, and Yosef all stood, clapping their hands as I entered the room. "Happy Birthday!" they all yelled.

"There was no need in this," I said, shyly.

"My girl," Viva said to me, "You are sveet sixteen. This day only come once. Tomorrow it vill all be back to normal."

Yosef took me in his arms. He was nineteen now. I looked into those deep, dark eyes of his, and I felt I had missed the moment he became a man.

"They are beautiful together," I heard Efraim say.

"Yes," Aunt Esther agreed.

Viva had begun cutting the birthday cake and placing slices on small plates that were chipped and browned. Quite certain her finest set.

"You are all so thoughtful," I kept telling them.

"Ah, I have forgotten something," Yosef announced.

"Vat? Forgotten? Vat have you forgotten?" His father not only stumbled over his words, but he almost lost his plate as he began patting his pockets as though the lost item might be there.

"The gift," Yosef answered. "I have forgotten her gift." He looked me in the eye. "I had wanted this to be perfect and here I have remembered everything except the most important part." He kissed my cheek. "I'll only be a minute."

He headed for a door that led upstairs to their apartment.

"Wait," I called to him. "I'll come with you."

"No," he said firmly. "I'll only be a minute." Then he disappeared up the stairs closing the door tightly behind him.

"He is ashamed," Viva said quietly, picking at her slice of cake.

"Ashamed?" Aunt Esther asked.

"He does not vant you to see that there is no chandelier hanging above our table." Viva shrugged her shoulders as she said this.

Aunt Esther shot me a look of surprise, then one of wonderment as if to say, "He really thinks we don't already know?"

"I have returned, gift in hand," Yosef said, bursting through the door. "This is for you, darling. Happy birthday."

I looked down into my hands. He had given me a small square box tied with ribbon. My mind started racing with the reality that this box was the perfect size to hold a ring.

"Come on . . . you're slower than a snail," he told me. "Open it already!"

With my mind swimming and my hands shaking, I untied the ribbon and let the paper drop to the floor. It was a ring box. "I knew it," said the voice in my head.

I slowly lifted the top of the box knowing that this moment, like my sixteenth birthday, would never come again.

"Well . . . say something!" he demanded.

"It's wonderful!" I forced myself to say. For inside the box lay one single ticket to a Broadway theater. My eyes were watering so that I could not read the title of the show.

"It's wonderful," I said again.

"It's me," he said.

"It's him," his father echoed.

"I made it. I made it to Broadway. I'm in this show. Next weekend is my debut."

It suddenly made sense. Yosef had been rehearsing extra-long hours for months and had acted secretive. He wanted to surprise me. I suddenly felt selfish and ungrateful. The only thing I could think to do was toss myself in his arms.

"I'm so proud of you," I whispered in his ear, my voice shaking.

"This is all so exciting!" I heard Aunt Esther say.

"What about you?" I asked, gesturing to his parents.

"Oh, ve'll be there, don't you vorry about us." Viva just smiled and patted her husband on the arm. "I vill make you something special to vear. My treat. For your birthday."

Later that night, as I lay in bed wiping tears from my cheeks, I regretted never telling Ida about this young man that had planted himself in my heart. I needed to share with her my silly assumption that he was going to propose. I needed to share with her the exact way my heart sank when there was no ring to be found inside the tiny box. But, how could I tell her now? After all these years, how could I tell her? And how could I tell Aunt Esther without her thinking me a silly child. No, I could never tell either of them. Instead, I took Miss Annie from the wardrobe where I had retired her some time ago. I straightened her hair and dress, placed her beside me in bed, and whispered my longings in her small porcelain ear.

16

I had seen Yosef perform in a number of small shows. But, performing on Broadway was a different matter altogether. Grand is the best word that comes to mind. The men all wore tuxedos, and the ladies wore precious jewels. Watching the couples sitting around me could have served as the show itself. But, when the curtains opened, my heart stopped. The lights filled my eyes, the music filled my soul, and when the dancers rushed the stage, my heart jump-started in my chest causing me to jerk and gasp for air.

His brow glistened with sweat as he moved in and out of the light. I felt my legs tingle, a sensation that scared and excited me. I felt my mouth open slightly as my breath hurried across my bottom lip. The drum began beating faster and faster, and his movements became harsh and aggressive. He began jumping in place and suddenly he tore a blue sash from his waist and tossed it into the air. A second later, the lights went out and I was startled by the applause around me. I spent every scene on the edge of my seat. I felt discontent when Yosef was not on stage. My emotions seemed uncontrollable and I feared crying. He was so powerful, so brave. Yosef seemed untouchable.

"Bravo!" I exclaimed, as I entered the greeting room. "You were spectacular."

"Thank you," he said, taking a bow. His confidence was almost overwhelming. He took my hand and kissed it. He smelled like the forest. He was beautiful.

"Tell me then. What was your take on this evening's performance?"

"It was . . . breathtaking," I answered. "I thoroughly enjoyed myself. I hardly think I'll sleep tonight. Such excitement. My heart is still pounding," I knew I was babbling and yet I couldn't stop myself. The more I spoke, the bigger his smile grew.

Yosef offered his arm, and I accepted. I would follow him anywhere. We walked the length of the hallway and entered a small room where there were two women sitting at a table, both with a cigarette in hand.

"Hey, Charlie," they both called. "Who's your gal pal?" asked the one in the red hat.

"This, ladies, is the very special, Maggie Fairchild."

"Good to meet you," they offered in unison. "I'm Roberta," said the owner of the red hat, "and this is Joan Weathers," she said, pointing to her friend, who was wearing a plaid skirt. Joan lifted her skirt, exposing a small flask strapped to her thigh. She winked at me as she lifted the flask, taking a slow drink of its liquid.

We continued through the room and out a back door, I couldn't help but stop and face him.

"I'm sorry, but did you just call me Maggie? And, what last name did you give me?"

"Listen, doll face," he whispered, "the beauty of the theater life is that life is literally an act. You can be anyone you want to be here. Take Joan for instance. Her real name is Thelma. But Thelma isn't a name you would expect to see written in the middle of a star, is it?"

"But, my name isn't written in a star."

"No, but does Delitha sound like someone Charlie would be seen with? No, Maggie is much more convincing."

"Who are we trying to convince?" I asked innocently.

"I'm growing tired of this game, my love." He leaned in and kissed me on the forehead. "Are you in a rush or would you accompany me to the 'after party'?"

"The after party?"

"Yes, well . . . it isn't really a party," he said, looking around. "Just a place where many of us, well . . . the better of us go after a night of performing."

"Where is this place?"

"Just a block over. Are you wearing your dancing shoes?"

"Well, I . . ."

Before I could answer, he had taken my hand and we were heading out a side door into an alley. There was steam coming from the grates in the streets. A dog could be heard in the distance. We seemed to be heading toward a dead end, and the walls appeared to be closing in on us.

"I don't think we should go any further," I whispered.

"Ah, don't be a flat tire."

"Excuse me?"

"Besides, we aren't going any further, we're here!" With that he opened a narrow door that a simple passerby would have never noticed. The door was opened less than an inch when the music from within hit us so hard I actually took a step back.

"Enter," he said smiling.

Directly inside the door was a small dark room holding one small table and a stool. On the stool was a young man with the brim of his hat concealing his eyes.

"Charlie, good to see you!" They embraced. "Who's this?" he asked, nodding at me.

"This, my friend, is the one and only, Maggie Fairchild."

"Hello," I said, forcing a smile. I was terrified.

"She looks harmless enough . . . take her on in."

Charlie opened the door and led me inside, his smile seemed to grow as the music surrounded us. My grip tightened around his arm.

"Take your eyes off me and look around!" he spoke directly into my ear. I stepped back and nodded.

It was overwhelming. The room itself was as large as the auditorium of the theater. Only where the theater was filled with rows of seating, this room was lined with tables all covered in half-empty glasses. The floor of the room was covered with young men and women . . . dancing. It was as if they all thought they were the only ones there . . . they all danced as if they were listening to their own song. The men were picking up the women and swinging them over their shoulders and under their legs, the women still standing were swinging their skirts scandalously high. The room smelled of sweat and alcohol. The room smelled of life. Charlie must have noticed the smile emerging on my face. He took my hand and gestured toward the floor.

"I've never danced like this before," I confessed, almost yelling for him to hear me.

"It's easy. You'll catch on in no time."

"Promise you won't laugh?"

"The only people that get laughed at here, are the ones standing still."

"Alright!" I yelled, throwing my hands up carelessly.

It was his feet I took note of first, although I quickly realized I wasn't meant to follow his steps. I set my eyes on the feet of the young gal next to me when Charlie took my chin in his hand. "They're all doin' their own thing . . . it's all about letting out the energy you've got pent up inside." He let go of my chin and spun around in a complete circle; his fingers began snapping and his head bobbed from side to side. "Let it all out!" he called for everyone to hear.

The music began vibrating in my bones, my skin began to tingle, and my soul let loose. My feet moved beneath my body in a way I never thought possible. I lifted my skirt exposing my knees and Charlie began to laugh out loud as he danced around me. "This is the moment," whispered a voice in my head, "this is the moment I want to live in . . . forever."

Outside, the streets were clear. Only the moonlight glared at us, and our laughter seemed to echo in the night.

"That was wonderful!" I exclaimed, taking his arm. "How did you find this place?"

"This place? Anyone who's anyone knows about this place." He smiled at me for a long moment. "But this isn't the only one, you know. No, I could take you to a dozen other scenes just like this one. Dancing, dancing, and more dancing. That's the only respectable thing to be doing these days, you know."

"I see." It was all I could think to say.

"You should have that Aunt of yours get you some dancing shoes. Real dancing shoes."

I had to admit, Charlie made a valid point. My toes were pulsing with my heartbeat and my ankles felt swollen. I would indeed be asking Aunt Esther for a pair of suitable dancing shoes, a request I felt certain she would love to fulfill.

"Dancing shoes?" she exclaimed. "I would love nothing more than to buy you a pair of dancing shoes! Two pair if you wish!"

"No, one pair will do."

I had just shared every moment of the prior evening with Aunt Esther; the show, Yosef changing our names, the dancing. I sat and bore my soul the way I imagine other girls do with their mothers or sisters. Aunt Esther was neither of those things, she was something better. Aunt Esther had become my best friend. With the exception of my desire for a proposal, I shared everything with her, every moment and I was still beaming. Beaming enough for Aunt Esther to see past the simple need for a pair of dancing shoes.

"You've fallen in love with him, haven't you?" she asked bluntly, catching me off guard. I sat with a blank expression, not wanting to answer the question.

"It's absolutely appropriate for you to love him. There's no need to be shy about it. It started out as puppy love and now it's the real thing. It's wonderful. Why are you blushing?"

"I am not blushing," I demanded, feeling my cheeks burn.

"Delitha, you came here a scared little girl, and somewhere between then and now you have become a strong, beautiful, independent young lady." She folded her arms across her chest and began tapping her fingers. "It's a simple question. Are you in love with him or are you not? Call me silly, but I just want to hear you say it."

"Yes," I whispered, unable to hide my smile.

"Bravo!" she called out, clapping her hands together. "Love is a wonderful thing."

She began to talk faster. "I knew it! I can smell it on you. You, my dear, reek of love." Aunt Esther took a deep breath and yelled with excitement, "Lillian, come here this instant!"

"Good heavens!" Lillian came puttering from the kitchen, wiping her hands on her apron. Sweat beads were glistening on her brow. When she made her way to Aunt Esther's side, she exclaimed, "My water's boilin' over. What's your matter?" Aunt Esther and I were so taken by the expression on her face, we both began to laugh, forgetting altogether why we had called her in. "Do the two of you want food in your bellies or have games become more important?" She stood before us with her legs spread and her fists on her round hips.

"Lillian, dear," Aunt Esther began, still trying to control her laughter. "There's no game here, I assure you. This is very serious, indeed!"

"I'll tell you what's serious," Lillian said, heading back for the kitchen door that was still swinging behind her, "your next meal, burnt and in the garbage. That's what."

Aunt Esther followed behind her, fanning her cheeks. "Lillian, wait. Be a dear and humor me for a moment."

Lillian turned to face us. "What?"

"Our little Delitha seems to have gone and fallen in love."

"What? Good heavens, child!"

Aunt Esther clasped her hands at her chest and cocked her head. "What shall we do with her?"

"Chop off her hair," Lillian offered.

"Excuse me?" I exclaimed.

"No, no, now hear me out. My grandmama used to say that when you found yourself wrapped up in love you should chop off your hair."

"What on earth for?" I asked covering my head with my hands.

"Well, child, I don't mean to shave your head. Just change it. Changing your hair can be a serious offense to a man, or it can be a great compliment. Change your hair; if he likes it, then you'll know it was meant to be. If he don't like it, well, then you'll know he ain't the one and you'll have a fancy new hairdo to help attract the next fella."

"What a splendid idea!" Aunt Esther said to herself, looking off into the air. "Yes, we'll do it together!"

17

Lillian had said that Charlie might be offended by me cutting my hair. But I knew he would welcome the change. My simple ways made Charlie stand out; made him the star of our show, which he loved. But, at the same time, when he called me Maggie Fairchild, we both knew I didn't fit the part. Charlie had worked so hard to get where he was, he deserved someone who was willing to work equally as hard to convince the world of who he was; who we were. This simple act, this cutting of my hair would not change me on the inside. But, the least I could do for him was look the part. Charlie would not be offended, he would take it as a compliment, I was sure of it.

Aunt Esther's favorite beauty parlor, Margaret's Boutique, was four blocks from her home. We walked there, arm in arm; a slight skip of excitement in our step.

"Delitha, you remember Margaret." Aunt Esther and Margaret embraced and exchanged pecks on the cheek. She turned her attention to me for a split second. "It's been a while since you've been here, hasn't it, Delitha?" Then back to Margaret. "Lillian has been trimming her hair at the house." They both turned and tipped their heads as they smiled at me. "But, today we have both come for a brand new look!"

"Ooh, that sounds wonderful!" Margaret exclaimed with wide eyes, "What sort of look are you hoping for?"

"I have three words that apply to the both of us." Margaret leaned in as if Aunt Esther had just offered to confess a lifelong secret. Aunt Esther took a deep breath and closed her eyes, "Off – with – it!"

They both stepped back and opened their mouths as wide as possible. I wasn't certain if it were to show horror or surprise.

"How wonderful!" Margaret reached out and took me under her arm. "Let's not waste another moment! To the chair!" she demanded. Aunt Esther, on cue, marched in and placed herself in a seat that might as well have had her name printed on it. She began removing pins from her bun as fast as her hands would allow.

"Delitha, make yourself at home. Isn't this exciting?"

Before I could answer, a different lady, not Margaret, had draped me in an off-white smock and was leading me to a seat opposite Aunt Esther. "Sit here," she said in a much too happy singsong voice. When I didn't respond as quickly as she had expected, she began to press down on my shoulders. "Just sit and relax. When I'm done with you, you'll look in the mirror and say, 'Who is that? Is that a movie star?'" She began running her fingers over my scalp.

"A movie star?" I asked her.

"Absolutely, the next time you look in this mirror, you'll be staring at a star." She spun my chair around away from the mirror and I began to play the word *star* over and over in my head.

"Charlie would love for me to look like a star," I said, smiling to myself, or at least I thought it was to myself.

"Charlie? Who's Charlie?" Margaret asked over her shoulder.

"Do you have a special someone?" asked the lady combing my hair. She leaned over and rested her chin on my shoulder. "Is he cute?"

"Handsome as everything!" answered Aunt Esther.

"Who is this mystery man?" Margaret inquired.

"You know the tailor shop on 34th . . . Demsky's?"

"Oh, yes. Very nice people, I buy all my hats there."

"It's their son."

"Their son?" asked Margaret turning to me. "I thought his name was Yosef."

"Charlie is his stage name, you know he's big time at the theater now"

"Why would he need a stage name? Oh, because they're Jewish."

Aunt Esther simply shook her head.

"Such a shame. Such a shame," Margaret said tugging at Aunt Esther's hair.

I suddenly felt confused. Aunt Esther had known they were Jewish. And that being Jewish meant he needed a stage name. Why had she not explained this to me earlier? Did she assume I knew? Did she think I had figured it out on my own, or perhaps that Yosef himself had explained the situation? Was this the real reason Yosef had changed his name to Charlie?

"And isn't it just so sad," Margaret began, "why, just the other day I heard about . . . " Aunt Esther interrupted her by simply placing her forefinger to her lips as if to shush her. "Right," Margaret said under her breath.

"What . . . what did you hear . . . just the other day you heard about . . .

what?" The woman deciding the fate of my hair, who still had not introduced herself, kept nagging Margaret until she finally gave in.

"I heard that Mr. Rice was forced out of business."

"Margaret, really." Aunt Esther waved her hand in the air as if to shoo away the words floating around her head.

"Really. He was forced to close."

"Margaret," Aunt Esther said again, this time more firmly.

"Who forced him? Can they do that?" asked Vera, I had finally noticed her nametag.

"Who?" asked a lady in the corner that I had not noticed before. She had metal rollers scattered about her head.

"Once it came out that they were Jewish, no one would buy from him; he was forced to close."

"Margaret," Aunt Esther said again, this time waving both hands.

"Rice doesn't sound Jewish," Loraine offered.

"It isn't . . . that's not his real name . . . it's Vladimir or something like that."

"Vladimir sounds Russian. Where did he come up with Rice?" Loraine asked, quickly chopping at my hair.

"It was all he had to his name when he arrived here. They asked him his name and rice was all that came to his mind."

"Are you talking about the shop around the corner, Rice's?" asked the lady in the corner.

"Yes, the older gentleman with the flower shop. Isn't it just so sad, what is this world coming too?"

"His name is Smyth," said the lady, plopping her magazine down on the table to her side. "He named his shop Rice's after his wife. That's her maiden name. He closed up because she has taken ill. And, they're Catholic, not Jewish."

"How do you know so much?" Margaret asked, taking a step back and putting her free hand on her hip.

"I'm married to their son. I am Alma Smyth."

Margaret stepped over to a small desk in front of the window and turned on a radio. "How about some music?" she asked, to no one in particular.

Alma Smyth stood and franticly began removing the rollers from her hair.

She slopped them one by one onto the floor and when she was finished she slowly walked over to the radio and turned it off.

"I can't wait to tell the ladies at my card club how I just found out that Margaret's Boutique is run by a Nazi. She's sure to be closed by Christmas." Alma Smyth turned the radio on again and with all the class she could muster, glided out the door with large curls bobbing about her head.

There was an outburst of laughter, overpowering the radio.

"That'll teach me then, won't it?" Margaret belted, laughing at herself in the mirror. "Let's finish you ladies up so you can be on your way. I have a reputation to uphold!" Again laugher echoed in the small room.

"You're being transformed," Aunt Esther said to me in a strained voice, trying to be heard over the music. "You're going to be gorgeous!" She began snapping her fingers to the beat. Margaret and Vera began swinging their hips as they moved around us. It was only a moment longer before I felt my own feet start to tap. Then my shoulders began to bounce a little. Before long we were all on our feet dancing, Aunt Esther and I still wrapped in our smocks with bits of hair flying about us. "Where are those dancing shoes when you need them?" I called out.

We danced around the room like mad women. We were acting undignified; like children. I closed my eyes and Ida appeared before me, dancing with all her might. Her cheeks were rosy, her hair tied up in ribbons. She was no more than ten years old. I could no more have imagined her at sixteen as I could have imagined myself looking like a star.

I felt a tug on my arm and I allowed Vera to lead me back to my seat. I sat just in time for her to spin me around. My eyes opened and the room whirled about me. When I came to a stop, I was facing the mirror. The girl staring back at me was unrecognizable. She was brilliant.

"This, my dear, is what we call a bob."

Dear Delitha,

I am writing with bad news. My mother has passed away. It was unexpected and I fear it has affected your family as much as my own. My father has not been out of his room since the service, three days now. I would have written sooner, but everything happened so fast. I spoke with your father today, he says your mother has been asking for her, but he cannot get her to understand what has happened. I admit, it is hard for even me to understand. Will I ever see you again?

Ida

My dearest friend,

I was heartbroken after reading your letter. I am so sorry to hear about your mother. Was she ill? I wish I had known. I realize that I could not have done much if I had returned, but I would like to have been there.

I feel so helpless, so far away. I would give anything to be with you right now. We could sit under Ol' Willy and cry together. But, I suppose we are too old for that now, aren't we? Now, I suppose we are expected to sit with handkerchiefs and console ourselves as adults do. Oh, Ida, is this what being an adult is all about? Not being there for one another? I feel so left out. Know that I am thinking of you and holding you in my heart. Oh, Ida, I am so very sorry.

Delitha

Del,

I'm certain you have heard of Mrs. Sunday. Her death was unexpected and she will be greatly missed. Your mother has been steady for some time now, but it seems the past week or so she has started to decline. She will not speak to me. I am not certain if her ability is gone or if she is simply refusing to interact. Perhaps seeing you would do her some good. I would like you to come home now. I miss you more than I can say. I try and imagine how much you have grown, how much you have changed. Come home, Del. I will make arrangements with Esther.

All my love,
Diddy

18

"Va-va-va-voom!" he yelled as I approached. Charlie was leaning against the wall outside his dressing room smoking a cigarette. "You look . . . you look . . . well, you look like a million dollars!"

He kissed me hard on the cheek and held me at arm's length. "Who did this to you? I want to thank them!" Before I could answer, we were interrupted by a large man wearing all black. And, although we were indoors, he was wearing dark sunshades.

"Who is this girl? I've seen her here before."

"This," Charlie answered, with emphasis, "is *the* Maggie Fairchild."

"Hello, Maggie Fairchild, glad to meet you." He offered his hand and I took it reluctantly. "Is this young man bothering you or are you here on your own free will?"

"I'm here on my own accord," I answered, with an unusual amount of confidence.

"Good, good. Good to hear it." He spoke quickly. "Listen, if you're going to be here, you might as well be working, understand? Find something useful to do or buy a ticket like everyone else."

"She works for me, bub. Didn't you know?" Just as Yosef began his lie, in walked the most beautiful woman I had ever seen. Her blonde hair was wavy and close to her head, her lips were large and ruby red, her skin white as snow.

"She's with you? What does she do for you?" asked the man in black.

"She's my personal assistant. Maggie assists my costume changes . . ." And before he could finish, the blonde beauty spoke, piercing me with her blue eyes.

"Ann called in sick, so today Maggie is being promoted to makeup artist." The blonde beauty puckered her lips rather than smiling.

"Ah, just find her something to do, will ya." He left Charlie's dressing room huffing under his breath.

"Come with me, kid. I'll show you the ropes," she said, wrapping her arm around me. "I'll give her back, don't worry." She smiled at Charlie and waved, "Ta ta."

Her dressing room was filled with lamps, dozens of them. They were all covered in brightly colored linens, sending different colored shadows all over the walls and ceiling. She had autographed pictures taped to her mirror, all of men, and none of whom I had ever seen or heard of.

"I'm Lizzy. Lizzy Gilespy."

"How do you do?" I asked.

"Fine. You are?"

"Delitha . . . I'm sorry, I mean, Maggie. Maggie Fairchild."

She walked a circle around me looking at me from top to bottom.

"I like you," she said. "I saw you dancing with Charlie at the club the other night. Your hair is much better this way. Do you know anything about makeup?"

"No, not stage makeup. I've only ever worn lipstick."

She smirked and then covered her mouth with the back of her first two fingers. "If you watch me do it tonight, do you think you could remember and do it for me tomorrow night?"

"Yes, ma'am. But don't you think . . . Ann . . . might be feeling better by then?"

"First of all, don't call me ma'am. It's Lizzy. Second of all, no. Ann didn't really call in sick. She called in to tell me that she and that no-good boyfriend of hers ran off to Reno." She pulled out a stool. "Shall we get started?"

Diddy,

I was deeply saddened to hear of Mrs. Sunday. I am also sad to hear of Mother's condition. Again, I think you should hire some help, give her someone other than yourself to rely on.

I regret telling you this, but coming home does not suit me at this time. I have many responsibilities here. Lillian is aging and has come to rely on me for help with her shopping and meal preparation. I am also volunteering at a local theater. I have been given a new respect for the arts, and leaving now would be walking out on the word I gave to help out. You do understand, don't you?

All my love to you,
Del

****

Lizzy and I became good friends. She shared stories with me, experiences that I had never even imagined possible. She was different than me. She wasn't what Lillian or Aunt Esther would have called a good girl. She was exciting and rebellious. She teased me for loving Charlie, a game between us that made me feel important. She respected Charlie, not just as a performer, but as a person. "He's a real gem," she would say. "He's a keeper." There were times when I felt as though she was envious of me. Envious because her relationships seemed to come and go, yet Charlie and I had been going strong and steady for years.

It was my eighteenth birthday and Charlie had planned a dinner party for him, me and Lizzy, along with whomever she had her nails into that week.

"This is Lonzo," she said, beaming as they stood before our table.

"Hello, good man. The name's Charlie. This is Maggie Fairchild."

"Good to meet you," I said, placing my cigarette on the edge of the ashtray long enough to shake his hand. As they took their seats, I took another puff and exhaled over my shoulder. A luxury, I had called it when Aunt Esther inquired of the scent, not a habit. It was Lizzy who had first offered me one. She said it was my reward for making her beautiful.

"So, this is for your birthday?" Lonzo asked without addressing me, as if he had already forgotten my name.

"Of course it's her birthday. I told you that on the way over." Lizzy not only scolded him verbally, but she reached under the table and swatted his leg.

"This is for you," Lizzy said, squinting her eyes and puckering her lips. "I hope you like it." She handed me a small box wrapped in white paper with a yellow ribbon.

"You didn't have to give me anything."

"Oh, don't be so modest," Charlie laughed kissing the side of my head. "You know you love getting gifts."

Inside the box, neatly folded, was a bright red, silk scarf covered with blackbirds.

"What on earth is it for?" Charlie pulled it out of my hands and began examining it.

"She knows what it's for. Give it back to her, you uncultured . . ."

"So, what did you get her?" Lonzo asked, as if he had always been part of our circle of friends. This question merited another swat from Lizzy. "He won't be around long," I thought to myself.

"Well, that's a good question . . . Lonzo." Charlie leaned back and propped his chair on its hind legs. He stayed in that position for an exaggerated amount of time before allowing his chair to smack back down on the floor.

"Let's see, what did I give you last year. Do you remember, doll face?"

"Of course I remember. You gave me my own makeup kit."

"What?" he exclaimed.

"That was from me!" Lizzy called out, pretending to be hurt.

I only smiled at her, "Charlie, you gave me this necklace."

I pulled it from beneath my collar, where the necklace my father gave me once rested. "I haven't taken it off." I told him.

"Good," he said, smiling. "I want to give you something else I hope you won't take off."

Lizzy slapped both hands over her mouth and Lonzo pulled her close as if she needed comforting. She jerked away and leaned forward to get a better view.

"This is for you, doll face."

It was a ring with a violet stone. It sparkled in the candlelight. It fit perfectly.

"I want everyone to know you're mine."

"Oh, Charlie!" It wasn't the proposal I was hoping for, but it would do. He had claimed me and I was thrilled to have a tangible symbol of our love. I embraced him tightly and went to kiss his lips, but he leaned his head back.

"You don't expect me to wear that red on my lips do you?" He kissed my cheeks instead. "Happy birthday, Maggie."

"Now let's really celebrate!" Lizzy pulled a small bottle from her bag and poured a bit into each of our drinks. "To Maggie! Now let's get zozzled!" she said, lifting her glass.

"To Maggie!" everyone repeated.

By the time Charlie walked me home, we had finished off Lizzy's bottle and had gone searching for more; much more. Lizzy and Lonzo had bid us good night and as they climbed into a taxi cab I could hear Lonzo chuckling as Lizzy loudly declared she was dangerously dizzy. Laughing uncontrollably, Charlie and I made our way to Aunt Esther's house with him guiding my steps as I stumbled to the front door.

"I love you," I whispered as I flung my arms around his neck.

"What's not to love?" he asked, cackling to himself.

"Will I see you tomorrow?"

With a slight slur he said, "Yes. My mother made you a dress for your birthday. Come by the shop, I'll take you to lunch."

Lunch. The thought of food made my stomach flip upside down. I stepped back not sure of what my body was about to do. "I don't feel so good."

"You'll feel better in the morning. Go inside and sleep, birthday girl."

I stood up straight and leaned against the front door. Before strolling away in the darkness, Charlie stepped into me and pressed his lips against mine.

I opened the door and was scolded by the lights. My hands instinctively covered my eyes. "How can I get to my room without uncovering my eyes?" I asked myself.

"Happy birthday!" came a voice from the kitchen.

"Happy birthday!" sang another.

"Too loud," I said, softly.

"Come in here, child. I gotta whip that tooshy of yours . . . eighteen times!" I peeked through my fingers, it was Lillian . . . she was waddling toward me holding a cake. The candles were leaving a trail of smoke as she walked.

"We've been waiting all night. Come open your gifts." Aunt Esther was at my side tugging at my sleeve.

"Don't act like you didn't know. Have we ever forgotten your birthday?" Aunt Esther pulled my hands from my face. She stepped back and stared at me with a blank expression. "You've been drinking," she said softly.

I had no response.

"Good heavens, child." Lillian came to my other side. They both peered at me with looks of disbelief.

"I need to lie down," I tried to push past them, but I fell into them instead.

"Delitha, what have you done?" Aunt Esther snapped.

"I had a birthday party," I answered, almost laughing. I stumbled to the bottom of the staircase. Looking up to the top made me dizzy. "Dizzy Lizzy," I said under my breath.

"Delitha, you come here and sit down," Aunt Esther demanded.

"I'm going to bed."

"Young lady, you come here!"

"No. I'm going to bed."

"Delitha!"

"You can't tell me what to do, Esther!"

"You are my responsibility, young lady."

I raised my hand to show off my ring. "I belong to him now." I turned to conquer the stairs.

"Delitha, what have you done?" Her voice was sad, distant.

"My name is not Delitha. It's Maggie. I am *the* Maggie Fairchild!"

"Good, that's good. Change your name. Change anything you want about yourself. But, don't do this! Don't turn into your mother!"

I felt a sudden surge of energy rush through my body and I bolted up the stairs as fast as my legs would carry me. To my surprise, Aunt Esther was at my heels and caught me by the arm when we reached the top. She spun me around. I could see Lillian standing at the bottom, she was hugging herself, there were tears streaming down her face.

"Delitha, do you not know what ails your mother? She is consumed with the drink. How could you not know this?"

I gasped for breath. It was as if someone had opened a window unexpectedly, slapping me in the face with freezing cold. But no breath would enter my lungs. My bedroom was only a few steps away; I turned to run, but Aunt Esther wrapped her arms around my waist tugging me in a direction my body did not want to go. I yelled at her to let me go. She held my waist as I kicked and screamed and twisted in her arms until we were both lying on the floor. Tired. Wet with sweat and tears. Forcing ourselves to breathe in and out.

When I woke, I was in my bed. I found myself curled up in a ball, facing Aunt Esther. She was in deep sleep, breathing slowly.

I leaned in and kissed her on the cheek, lingering for a moment, feeling her breath on my own cheek, feeling her soft skin rise and fall with each breath. It was still dark, and it seemed as though time did not exist, as I drifted in and out of sleep. I didn't come to full consciousness until I was startled by a cold, wet rag on my forehead.

"I didn't mean to wake you," she said softly. "You were hot."

There was nothing to say. I felt ashamed for the way I had acted and humbled that she was still willing to care for me.

"You know, Delitha. Your mother is not all bad. You are the best part of her . . . I wish you could have known her before . . . well, people used to say your mother hung the moon. I always said she *was* the moon. The light inside of her shone through even on the gloomiest of days. Her laughter was musical, her smile a work of art. I remember the day your parents announced their engagement. I was always envious of her."

"Envious?" I whispered. "Of her?" I closed my eyes again, nauseous.

She let out a nervous, regretful laugh before speaking.

"No man has ever loved me the way your father loves her."

I squinted enough to see that her eyes were fixed on a loose thread sticking out from my quilt. Her jaw was clenched.

"It's funny really, when you think about it," I said.

"Funny?"

"You've spent years being envious of the same person that I've spent years despising."

"Hmm . . . that is rather funny isn't it?" She stood and moved to the door, leaving the rag on my head. "Delitha, we can . . . hope . . . that when you return home you will find your mother to be what she once was. One day, I hope, you will agree that she hung the moon." She quietly shut the door and hesitated before walking away.

"The moon," I said, leaning over to see out my window into the night sky. "Not my moon."

I tugged at my pocket until I retrieved the scarf that Lizzy had given me only hours before. I draped it over my lamp and stared at the shadows until I was once again overtaken by sleep.

Morning came much too soon. My body felt weak and limp. A noise from outside caught my attention. At the window I could see the mail carrier mounting his bicycle. To my surprise, it was not morning. It was mid-afternoon. I fumbled through my wardrobe for several minutes before deciding not to change my clothes. My water basin was full, and the cool water sent goose bumps over my body. There were circles under my eyes, dark ones. My face was swollen and it took effort to get control over my hair. It was the first time in years that I saw Mother looking back at me in the mirror. "Don't you turn into your mother!" I remembered hearing Aunt Esther say. I didn't want to. My stomach was in knots, and my skin felt as though it might fall off and leave me with only my bones, and those were feeling too weak to hold me up. I made no concessions that morning. I did, however, make a promise, though not so much to myself. I made a promise to any children I might bear later in life. I promised that I wouldn't be like Mother, so that one day they might say, I hung the moon.

As I emerged from my room, I heard what sounded like crying, then whispers, then more crying. I gripped the railing best I could to get myself down the stairs. There was no one to be seen when I reached the foyer. My head turned instinctively as I heard voices from the kitchen.

"Should I wake her?"

"No, she'll be up soon enough."

I walked to the door, thankful the lights were low. As I swung the door open, I found Lillian standing at the cupboard, staring inside as though she had forgotten what she was looking for. Aunt Esther was seated at the table, her head in her hands.

"Is anything the matter?" I asked, startling them both.

"Good heavens, child. You are bound and determined to kill me."

"I'm sorry, Lillian. I didn't mean to sneak."

Lillian and Aunt Esther exchanged glances.

"Sit down, dear heart," Aunt Esther said, forcing a smile. "This came for you." She held up a telegram. "I hope you don't mind. I took the liberty of opening it. I knew it was from your father and I didn't know how long you would be in bed. I guess I long for his letters as much as you . . . you know he always includes a note to me."

"You don't have to explain," I said, just wanting her to stop talking and thereby stop the pounding in my head.

She pushed the envelope across the table to where I was sitting.

"I'll read it later if it's all the same to you."

"Delitha, it's your mother." Her lip began to twitch. "She's . . . she's . . . gone."

"Why now?" I thought to myself. This is so like her. It seemed to me as if this were her one last selfish move. She had to do this so that the news would get to me on the one day I myself felt like dying. I hated her.

"There is no doubt you should attend the service. There is a train leaving at four. Can you be ready by then?"

"Yes," I said, shaking my head in disbelief.

"Would you like to share a trunk, or will you be needing one of your own?"

I knew what she was asking. Would I be staying in Georgia or returning to New York with her.

"No," I answered. "We can share."

Lillian walked over and placed her hand on Aunt Esther's shoulder.

"This should be recorded in the family Bible."

"Thank you for reminding me, Lillian. I'll do that now."

"I'll do it," I said, surprising myself. Nothing else was said as I stood from the table and shuffled to the door. "I was planning to meet Charlie today for lunch. I've missed it, haven't I?"

"I'll send word on what has happened," Aunt Esther assured me. "Should I let him know he is welcome to accompany you home?"

I did not answer her.

Aunt Esther's library was full of books that no one ever read. There was a desk that no one ever sat at. In the corner, sitting high on a pedestal was the Hancock Family Bible. It was bound in brown leather and quite beautiful. I remember looking at it when I first arrived. My parents' wedding had been recorded there, and my birth and baptism. It was the only tangible thing binding my family together.

I opened the Good Book, expecting to be hit by a cloud of dust. Instead, I was hit by a small folded piece of paper that floated down and landed on my foot. My head was spinning as I bent over to pick it up. My intention was not to be nosey. In fact, I had no thoughts at all as I unfolded the paper. To my surprise, it was in my diddy's handwriting.

My loving sister, Esther,

Simply writing the letters in your name has given me a sense of hope; a feeling I have almost forgotten. Esther, we are desperate. Our lives have been sliding downhill for some time now, and at last we have hit bottom. Beverly has not seen outside our bedroom in weeks. Her addiction is no longer controllable and I have no one to blame but myself. In all my years as a husband - as a father- I have never before felt a failure. But now, I fear there is no other word to describe myself. I have failed. I have failed my wife, my daughter, and myself. I have even failed you. My simply asking you for help is a sign that I have not fulfilled my responsibility to be the older, wiser, brother. I have failed miserably at the task set before me.

I have allowed Beverly the very indulgence that will surely take her life. And Delitha, my dear Del, how I have failed her! The sparkle that once danced in her eyes now lies dormant in a hollow tomb. The unstoppable optimism I have always admired in her has faded to an understandable hopelessness. She is nothing more than an abandoned shell, following behind her father, desperately picking up the pieces he drops as he runs to hide from the hell he has created.

I am tired of hiding, Esther. There is nothing left for me to do but face what I have allowed to happen. I am begging for your good graces, sister. I ask with a humble heart that you would take Delitha under your wing. Her need for a mother is unmistakable. She needs love and attention and nourishment of every kind. She needs more than I can give her.

My vow is to Beverly. I still remember how the words "in sickness and in health" felt rolling off my tongue. I vowed to honor her. To love her. I never imagined I could fail so miserably.

You are my only hope, Esther. If you will revive Delitha, perhaps I can do the same for my wife. My only comfort is the hope of our family coming back to life. And you, Esther, are a vital part of our recovery. Please do not deny me this chance to fix what I have broken. Allow me this chance to make my wrongs right.

Please, Esther. Help us out of this pit we have fallen into. Give our Delitha the life she deserves. Mold her into the woman I know she can become. Please, Esther, bless us with your good graces.

Your brother,
Walter

I folded the letter and placed it back in the book. I never recorded Mother's death. My mind was swimming as I walked back to my room. Everything seemed different. Even the air smelled different. It was then that I realized my Aunt Esther had not come like an angel to save me. Instead, my father had given me away. I had not been rescued; I had been sent.

19

I'm not certain what I expected. Rain I suppose. But it was unseasonably warm. The sky was well lit, with large shoots of sunshine breaking through the clouds. There was no breeze. Everything seemed to be standing still. Especially my diddy. He stood before the box that held her body, standing as lifeless as she lay. The silence said more than any words he could have used. He had lost his wife, his friend, and the mother of his only child. And above all, he blamed himself. What could he have said?

It seemed that I was the only one with dry eyes. Even Aunt Esther alternated her handkerchief from the corner of her eye to her nose. I suppose I was mourning too, in my own way, in my heart and in my mind. But I felt, just as I had for years, that I had already shed enough tears over her. That day was no exception.

There were no tears. But that doesn't mean there were no emotions. I felt something. Emptiness and confusion. As if something had been stolen from me. Something that, until it was gone, I hadn't realized was dear to me. Was it Mother I had finally placed value on? I don't think so. I think it was the time. As long as Mother was sick, I knew what life held for me. I knew that Aunt Esther was my life. My constant. Now, with Mother in the ground, there was nothing binding me to Aunt Esther and the life I had made in New York. I felt angry at her. At Mother. Angry because now I would have to choose. The choice was once made for me, but now, the choice was mine.

Mine. A word that has never fit with me. Even in the lavish love of my Aunt Esther, I had never felt that anything was truly mine. All mine. Mine in the sense that I had chosen it. That I had selected it. That I had sought it out and made it my own. Made it mine.

Finally, after all these years, Mother had afforded me that chance. The chance to choose. The chance to make myself, my own. There was my diddy and the chance to start a new life with him in Georgia. For him, perhaps it would simply be moving on. But, for me, it would be starting over. On the other hand, there was Aunt Esther. I could choose to return to New York with her and allow her to finish the job she had started. The transformation she had begun on me the moment we first met. I would then be free to continue leading the life to which Yosef and I had become so accustomed. I was free to choose. I had waited for this day, this burial, my entire life. And now that it was before me, freedom felt a million miles away. The choice I now faced, the freedom I now had to choose for myself, was weakening. My true, no-strings-attached freedom, left me feeling like a prisoner.

My diddy, Aunt Esther, and I stood in front with our backs to the crowd. I wondered if Ida was there, yet I didn't have the energy to turn and look.

After the service, we moved to a spot just past the burial site and shook hands with all those who came to pay their respects. Many of the people I knew. People that, at one time, I could have drawn their picture from memory. People I looked at now, after a six year absence, and could hardly call forth their names. Among the crowd were also folks that had stayed at the inn. Folks that traveled from surrounding towns to say thank you, one more time, to the lady that had taken them in and filled their bellies.

"Look at you," she said to me.

"I beg your pardon."

"Look at you," she said again.

I felt shame that I did not recognize her immediately.

"Ida," I said throwing my arms around her. "I hoped you would be here."

"Why would I not be here?" She stepped back to look me over again. "Would you like to take a walk?"

We walked with a small distance between us. Every few steps Ida would turn her head and look at me.

"What?" I finally asked her.

"Look at you!" she said again. "You aren't you."

"I'm not me?"

"I knew you would change while you were gone, but this . . ." She waved her hand at me. "It's just strange. When I look at you and then back at myself . . . well, it's obvious which one of us has spent time in the city and which one stayed in the sticks."

She reached up and puffed my hair.

"It's so short," she said in disapproval.

"It's the style," I told her.

"In the city," she said, making her point.

We approached a large tree that had fallen and we sat on the hollow trunk. "How are you?" she asked, resting her hand on my back.

"I'm not sure," I answered. "Tomorrow will be a better day."

"Yes, tomorrow will be a better day," she agreed. "I'm just curious," she removed her hand and scooted over a bit. "Will you be staying, now that you're here?" I sat silent for a moment before I answered, thinking about my words before they came out. "I had planned to return with Aunt Esther."

She sighed and looked away.

"But, now that I'm here, I think my diddy needs me to stay a while."

A shiver shot down my spine. The words I was thinking and the words that came from my mouth were completely different.

I sat for a moment trying hard not to speak, but the words came from me as if some greater force had taken control of my tongue.

"Have you seen inside that house?" I asked her. "I doubt he's lifted a finger outside of Mother's room since I left. I can't leave him in that mess. Who knows, it could take me a year to get that house back in order."

"A year?" I asked myself. "Shut up!" I screamed inside my head.

"I have a surprise for you," Ida said, getting back on her feet.

"Okay. Surprise me," I said, thankful for her to take control of the conversation.

"Robert Lansing has asked me to marry him. Can you believe it?" she yelled.

"I'm so happy for you! When did this happen?"

"Just last week. My next letter to you was going to be an announcement."

She looked so beautiful with her wide smile and the sun skipping across her face. "Will you stay?" she asked. "We were planning on next month. I know it's quick, but that's what works . . . will you please stay. I want you here so badly."

"Will I stay?" I asked myself "Will I stay? For a month?"

I thought for a moment and decided a month was better than a year.

"Yes," I promised her. "I wouldn't miss your wedding for the world!"

Aunt Esther turned in early. My diddy planted himself in his office and had not shown his face in over five hours. I took a risk in disturbing him.

"May I come in?" I knocked gently on the door and it opened slightly as it had not been latched.

"Come in," he whispered.

He was standing at the window, looking aimlessly at the night sky.

"I thought you might like some coffee." I spoke in a voice that was not my own. It seemed softer and more compassionate than the one I had been given. When he did not take the cup I offered him, I sat it on his desk.

My hand slipped and the cup landed on the saucer with a clank bringing him out of his trance. He shuffled to his desk, reaching for the steaming cup.

"Thank you, Del."

He finished his coffee before either of us spoke. As usual, he spoke first.

"My sister tells me you have taken up with a Jewish boy." The tone in his voice made me immediately defensive. "Does he have a name?"

"She didn't tell you his name? Only that he is Jewish?"

"She told me that this boy has grown from a playmate to a companion. The real question is why you never mentioned him to me."

He glared at me over his glasses and rubbed his cheek with his forefinger. "His name is Yosef," I told him. "I wanted him all to myself," I wanted to say.

"Tell me about him. Esther says you are quite smitten."

I suddenly felt betrayed.

"He is a good man. He comes from a hardworking family. His parents own a store in the city. His father is a tailor. His mother makes hats and dresses. She is quite talented. Aunt Esther is a customer there. That's how we met."

"Ah," he said quickly. "So, Yosef works with his family. He is a tailor as well."

It was a trap. He knew my answer before I gave it.

"No," I sighed. "Yosef is a performer. He's a dancer." There was a forced confidence in my voice.

"Del, I think you know where I'm going with this." He leaned forward and rested his elbows on his knees, clasping his hands in front of him. "You're smarter than that, Del."

"Smarter than what?" I leaned back resting my hands in my lap, feeling my cheeks begin to redden.

"Del, you can't give the rest of your life to a . . ." he hesitated as if he couldn't even say the word. "A . . . a dancer. He will not have the resources to care for you and a family."

"Haven't you always said that where there is love, there is enough?"

He stood and walked toward me, placing his hands in his pockets and straining to keep them there.

"Delitha, love doesn't put food on the table. Love doesn't put a shirt on your back." He gave in to letting his hands flail around him. "You will not return to him. Do you understand me?"

I stood and met him. He picked up his Bible and began fanning the pages.

"Whether I return to him or not is my decision and mine alone."

"I should have never trusted Esther with you," he yelled, pointing his long finger at me. "She knows nothing of raising children. I sent you there for guidance, and she shows you how to throw your life away."

"It wasn't much different from living here. Mother drank my life away!"

Before I drew my next breath, I was sent to the floor, my face burning.

My father stood over me. One hand fisted and the other gripping the Good Book. I tasted blood. There was no feeling in my lip. When he finally stepped back, I rose, shaking. I stumbled across the room and placed my hand on the door knob.

"I didn't raise you to turn your back on this family." His voice was low, sinister. I turned to meet his gaze, catching a glimpse of blood on my sleeve.

Despite my racing heart, I kept my voice steady. I wasn't surprised by the look on his face when I reminded him, "You didn't raise me."

It wasn't until the next morning that I felt the sting of God's Word. My lip was broken, blue, and swollen beyond its boundary. My chin was tender to the touch, yet I gave in to the temptation to press on it. I hesitated before entering the kitchen. I wasn't certain how to address the man that had set me in such a state.

"Del, is that you?" His voice was low, tired.

"Yes, Father."

I swung open the door to find him hunched over a cup of coffee, his head in his hands, his eyes closed. I moved to the cupboard and removed a cup for myself. I moved around the room with my back to him. After filling my cup, I stood in front of the sink resting my free hand on its edge. It tasted the way dirt smelled. He had never been good at brewing coffee.

"You've never called me that before," he whispered.

"Called you what?"

"You called me father. I guess I should have known that one day you'd be too grown up to call me diddy." He removed his glasses and rubbed his eyes.

I stood silent, sipping my liquid dirt, forcing it down with hard swallows.

"I can't tell you how sorry I am." I heard his cup clank the side of his saucer as he raised and lowered it. "I am a broken man, Del. It's more evident to me every day." His breath was audible. "I will not make excuses for my behavior." He rose from his seat and moved to my side. "You are not my little girl anymore." He brushed my hair with his hand. "You are a woman now. Your life is your own." He stepped back for a moment before bending at the waist and allowing his tears to flow freely. "Will you forgive me?" he cried. "Will you please forgive me?"

I caught him and we sank to the floor in each other's arms. I held him as he cried and I began to understand that his anger was not for me. Perhaps it was for Mother, perhaps the Lord. Perhaps himself. He was broken. In more ways than one.

Although we spent the day in the same house, we were further apart than ever. I had forgiven him, and he me. Yet, there was something different between us. Something had changed since the night before. Perhaps a bond had been broken, or merely replaced. Perhaps a trust, a security had been erased. Whatever it was, it filled the house and left us empty. Aunt Esther felt it as well. She moved about the house like a ghost, tending only to herself.

Long after the crickets began their evening concert, I prepared a small meal and the three of us dined in silence. Aunt Esther pretended to ignore my swollen lip. My father never made eye contact with either of us. Afterwards, Aunt Esther returned to her room and I moved to the front porch for air. After what seemed like an eternity, my father joined me. It wasn't until then that he broke the silence.

"The true love affair, the one I am truly concerned about, is between you and that city."

"I beg your pardon?"

"If Yosef has truly won your heart, then you should go to him." He stood next to me. His eyes were swollen; his nose stuffy. "I'm just not certain that he is the one that has stolen your heart. I believe it is the city itself. This way of life you never knew existed. The lights, the people, the quick pace in which everyone lives their lives. This is the culprit."

"The culprit?" My heart began to race and my skin went numb.

"Listen to me." He turned my face toward him. His earlier apology seemed void. "Let an old man give you a word of advice." His eyes drifted down to my lip as he spoke. "The excitement of the city, of the theater is . . . " He looked up at the velvet sky trying to find his words. "It's magical. You can't find that kind of energy anywhere else. When you're young, you're full of energy and you crave magic. You can run from here to there and make sense of the whirlwind in which you're living. Many find great happiness there, living and dying in the limelight." He pressed his hair down with both hands. "Delitha, what I'm trying to say is that . . ." He took a deep breath, in and out. "No matter where you live, there will come a point in your life where you will find happiness in your home. You will find energy in your partner and you will find magic in the eyes of your children." Deep breath, in and out. "If that life is waiting for you in New York, I would be a fool to try and keep you from it."

He briefly touched my shoulder with his hand then went back in the house. The anger inside me was pressing against my skin, desperately trying to break through. I had to get away. Not just away from my father, the house, the memories, and the advice. I had to get away from myself. Away from the very skin that held my body together. I began to walk . . . down the path, through the gate, and onto the walkway that lay between the homes and the road. My walk began to hasten. By the time I passed the gate to Ida's home, I was running with all my might, rushing at the night air like a warrior going into battle. No sounds could be heard over my heart, beating like a drum inside my head. My chest burned. My legs tingled and threatened to go limp with every step. A combination of sweat and tears covered my face, my chest. I had run past three estates when I came to a bend in the road. My arm scratched against a row of bushes as I turned the corner. My breath was stolen from me as I hit what felt like a brick wall and fell backward onto the ground. I shook my head and opened my eyes.

"Pardon me, miss. Are you hurt?"

He knelt next to me and placed an extra large hand behind my head, raising it from the ground. His voice seemed strangely familiar, yet I could not place it. There was no light to show his face, only his silhouette illuminated in the moonlight. "Miss, let me help you up. Are you able to stand?"

"I . . . I . . ." my thoughts were as jostled as my body.

"Lift your arm, let me help you."

This man, this body of steel, slid one arm under my upper body and one under my knees. He raised me from the earth. My head rested on his shoulder with an ease I had never felt. I could feel his heartbeat on my side. He took long strides, carrying me with no effort. I seemed to be floating.

"Can you tell me your name, miss? Do you live near here?"

I heard his questions, but I was unable to answer. I had drifted into a state of . . . was it shock? My eyes would not open, my mouth would not move. Exhaustion came over me like a winter's wind--unexpected and overwhelming, but necessary. My mind immediately shifted to a dream-state, placing me back home in my feather bed on the second floor of Aunt Esther's house. I felt the weight of grandmother's crazy quilt pressing on my body. The warmth of Aunt Esther's hand on my cheek.

"Delitha." At the sound of her voice, I willed my eyes to open, expecting to see her sitting next to me. She would be draped in her satin robe, smiling down on me with her enormous smile. "Delitha."

To my surprise, it was not Aunt Esther smiling down on me. I blinked heavily, once, then twice, trying to bring the masculine figure into focus. Then, after a moment, his identity became clear. Ida's father knelt on the floor beside the sofa. His face was at an uncomfortable distance from my own. His eyes were as brown as molasses; a trait of his I had never been close enough to admire. He looked down on me the way, I suspect; he looked down on his wife when she needed comfort. Perhaps the way he looked down on her as she looked past his eyes and into the light.

"When you are able, I will gladly help you home." His voice carried like a leaf in the wind. "Are you hurting?"

"No . . . I'm quite alright, thank you."

"What were you running from?"

"Myself." I raised my head, then lowered it again with a breathtaking pain through my shoulders.

"Take it easy, Delitha" He placed one hand on my forehead, the other by my side. Hearing my name spoken in his deep, raspy voice gave me chills.

For a reason I could not yet explain, I was both pleased and embarrassed that he recognized me.

"You must think me frightful." I closed my eyes. "My running into you, carrying on in such a manner."

"Were you successful?"

"I beg your pardon?"

"Were you able to escape yourself?"

Still unable to collect my thoughts or my words, I opened my eyes to find him smiling at me. My mouth, in a natural response, began to curve up at the corners.

"No, I suppose I did not succeed. I am still very much here, with myself, aren't I?"

"Yes, you are," he chuckled. "And your lip, did yourself do that to you?"

"No, my father did that."

His smile retreated.

"Oh, it's not what you think, really." I attempted once more to lift my head.

He held up his hand and leaned back. "You don't have to explain this to me. I am a father too, you know. I've lost my temper and made my share of mistakes as well."

"How are your children, if I might ask?" I was happy for a reason to change the subject.

"You may," he said, rising to his feet. "The boys are all living their lives. Far away from here." He moved to a small rocking chair and crossed his legs as he sat. "Ida will be leaving me soon, I'm certain she told you of her engagement. Robert is a good man. I know he will be good to her."

He rocked slowly, back and forth, his shadow following him. Back and forth, back and forth.

"Where is Ida?" I asked quietly.

"Oh, well, she's sleeping. I can wake her if you'd like."

"No, no there's no need. Thank you."

"Will you be returning home?" he asked.

"Of course, I mean, I can't stay here . . ."

"No, I'm asking if you'll be returning to New York."

"Oh." I lowered my head, blushing. "Yes, I suppose I will . . . I mean, I . . .

plan to stay for the wedding, but after that . . ." I could no longer look him in eye. I dropped my feet to the floor, which unexpectedly brought him to my side.

"May I help you home, to your father's house, I mean?"

"It isn't necessary, really." He took my arm and guided me to my feet, which at last were supporting my weight.

"Let me be a gentleman," his breath played upon my cheek. "It's been a while since I've had the chance."

He linked my arm in his and allowed me to lean on him while we walked. We were silent until we reached Father's front door. He moved his free hand to my arm and the other to my back, supporting me as I shuffled up the stairs that hid themselves in the shadow of the night sky.

"Thank you. Tell Ida I will try and see her tomorrow."

"She'll like that," he said softly.

"Good night," I whispered. I saw my father's shadow cross the foyer from the corner of my eye.

"Good night." He moved to the bottom step before turning back. "If you decide to run from yourself again tomorrow evening, I suggest you take Ida with you. There's safety in numbers."

I brought my giggle to a sudden halt when I realized how childish it sounded.

"Yes, sir."

He bent ever so slightly at the waist as he began to walk away.

"You're a woman now, Delitha. You may call me John."

20

Morning found me on the edge of my bed anxiously awaiting its arrival, as if the fresh light granted me permission to begin my day. My heart and stomach were set on cranberry biscuits, the kind Lillian made. Although she had never given me her recipe, I had seen her work her magic enough times to feel comfortable trying it myself. That morning, for the first time ever in that house, I felt at home. I moved about the kitchen as if it were, and always had been, mine. I prepared breakfast as though it had been my routine for a lifetime. There was a freedom in my soul.

The coffee had been brewing long enough to drift its scent up the staircase, under my father's covers and around Aunt Esther's nightcap. It beckoned them to surrender their sleep to consume its black magic. Their footsteps could not be heard, only the creak of the boards on which they placed their steps.

One by one, my father's footsteps inched closer to the kitchen till the creaking halted and the door swung open. Although he hunched his shoulders, his face looked rested. He raised his hand to pet my back, but I moved before he reached me. Untying the apron from behind me was the biggest challenge of the morning. Father, without hesitation, separated my hands, then the knot.

"Your mother had a habit of tying her apron too tight." He said. I turned to face him. "That's something I never imagined missing." He raised his hand and placed it on my cheek. I allowed him to hold it there. His hands were rough, uninviting. So much about him had changed. His thick, dark hair was now thinning and patching itself with gray. His nose had thinned as well, causing him to push up his glasses if he should tilt his head down. Yet, with all the changes, he was still the man I once knew. His heart had not changed. Even though the changes I had undergone were forcing me to call him Father, he was and forever would be, my diddy.

He stepped away from me with his hand still raised, cupped as if my face were still in it.

"Are you hungry?" I asked.

He lowered his arm in slow motion as he turned to face the table.

"My goodness. There's enough here to feed an army."

He pulled out his chair, sat, and scooted himself to the table having never taken his eyes off the meal laid out before him. I placed a plate before him just in time to catch the crumbs falling from his mouth. He had eaten half a biscuit in one bite.

"I don't believe I've eaten much the past few days," he placed the remaining half in his mouth and managed to spit out the words, "Perhaps months."

It was his confession that drew my attention to his attire. His clothing hung off him as it would a child playing dress-up in his father's suit. He looked poor as he sat there devouring his meal, like a beggar draped in a donation from a rich man with a heavy heart.

"Don't stare at them. They are not for entertainment," Aunt Esther's voice rang in my head like the church bell from my youth. I moved to the window, allowing father to nourish himself out from under my watchful eye. He ate quickly and stopped only when he needed to catch his breath. This went on until his plate had been cleaned twice and the color in his face had been restored. He retrieved the morning paper and a fresh cup of coffee. He remained at the table, I at the window. What news my father was reading of I did not know, nor care to know. My eyes were set on the home next door. The porch had been freshly painted and it almost sparkled in the morning light. The window boxes were all hanging straight, filled with color and life.

"How did she die?"

"I beg your pardon?"

"How did Carolyn die? Don't you know?"

"Yes, I do. Forgive me, Delitha, the death of one's neighbor is not typically a conversation shared over breakfast."

"You're right," I said apologetically.

He went back to his coffee and paper. Every few minutes he would pause, somehow finding more room in his gut to take another bite.

"It's just that . . ." He tilted his paper down just enough to show his eyes peeking over top. "Ida wrote to me of her mother's death, but with no real explanation. I admit, I never thought much of it till now. It just seems a bit strange, that's all."

He didn't answer me right away, taking time to finish the article he had started. At last he folded the paper, set it to the side, and turned his body to rest one ankle upon his other knee.

"She was with child."

I could not stop my eyebrows from raising.

"Her body was too tired. She had labored for some time before John came and asked me to come and pray over her. The doctor couldn't stop the bleeding. Nor could he put air into the baby's lungs."

"And you prayed over her?" I asked, stunned.

"I prayed over her before and after she passed. The good doctor could not save them, and the Good Lord chose not to. It was their time, Delitha." He uncrossed his leg and turned back to the table. "She was a good woman and the baby was beautiful."

A mental picture of them flashed through my head; I closed my eyes, willing it away.

"What will he do once Ida is married?"

"I imagine he'll be lonely." Father spoke with a knowledge I had yet to acquire.

"Do you think he'll move back to the country?"

Rather than answering my question, he pointed to a second basket of biscuits. "You should take these over. Ida has really missed you. Go and visit, I'll be fine here. Esther will keep me company."

"Are you sure?"

"Go," he urged, taking another look at the remaining food.

I picked up the second basket and headed for the door.

"Del," Father called to me as the door swung open. "It is so good to have you home." Although I did not look his way as I left the room, I could feel his eyes, and smile, upon me.

"Where are you off to this morning?"

I turned to find Aunt Esther coming down the stairs.

"I'm going to visit Ida."

She came to me and uncovered the basket that sat in my hands.

"Why, these look like Lillian's biscuits." She leaned in and sniffed them.

"You little thief," she smiled, "you stole her prize-winning recipe!"

"Be a dear and don't tell her," I said, something I had heard her say a million times.

"My lips are sealed."

"Esther!" my father called from the kitchen. "Come eat before all this good food goes to waste!"

She moved toward the kitchen door, still smiling. She blew me a kiss before we parted ways, she to the kitchen, I to our neighbors.

"Well, good morning," John said, stepping out onto the porch. His shirttail was untucked on one side and he was not yet shaven. Surprisingly, he looked younger than he had the night before.

"Good morning. My batch of biscuits turned into two batches . . . I thought you and Ida might enjoy some."

"Well, it's about time you came knockin' on my door!" Ida came from behind her father and wrapped her arms around me. "Oh, I've missed you."

Her father stood smiling at us. "Come, come inside," she said, taking my hand.

The house looked different in the daylight. It was beautiful. The more I looked around, the more I realized how filthy my father's house had become.

"Would you like to eat outside? Under the gazebo?" I asked her, suddenly needing some fresh air.

She set out a handful of biscuits for her father, then handed me the half-empty basket. "Follow me," she said, smiling.

"What happened to your lip?" She finally asked.

"Oh, well…you know, the house is so unfamiliar now. I was up last night and tripped over a small table that I didn't remember being there. The next thing I knew, I was face down on the hardwood."

Ida was smart enough not to believe my story, but she was friend enough to let me lie.

"Did your father tell you about last night?" I asked, letting out a nervous laugh.

"No. What about last night?"

"He didn't tell you?" I asked, surprised.

"Tell me what?"

"Well…we were both out for a walk and I guess you could say we sort of bumped into each other."

"That's strange. He didn't mention it." She shrugged her shoulders. "But, you know, he's been very distant since my mother died." She picked up a biscuit. "How's your father?"

"Well, he isn't distant." I said licking my fat lip.

"They all grieve differently." She said, as if she had witnessed the healing of a dozen widowers.

"How was she?" I asked, surprising myself.

"She, who?"

"Mother. Did you see her at all near the end?"

"No." She said, sadly. "Your mother would only have two people in her room, your father and my mother. I tried once. Your father had gone out to get more medication. My mother was feeling ill and asked me to look in on her. When I opened her door she seemed fine, she was staring at the window, only the curtains were pulled. Without thinking, I drew the curtains back, and the instant the light touched her face she . . . you don't want to hear this."

"Yes, I do. Please Ida. I've missed so much, I feel completely shut out."

Ida sat for a moment, fighting tears.

"She went crazy. I've never seen anything like it. She was like a wild animal. I had no idea . . . ." She stopped to steady her breath and wipe a tear from her lashes. "I was so scared. I left her. I ran home. My momma went over and . . . well, we never spoke of it again and I never went back."

"I'm so sorry you had to see that, Ida."

"I'm sorry." She said back to me. "I spent so many years being so angry at your parents . . . and at you. I couldn't understand why you had to leave. But, that day, that day I understood."

21

"Come in." I said softly. It was well into the night, yet there was a soft knock at my door.

"I saw your light." Aunt Esther whispered as she peeked in.

"I can't sleep." I patted the bed next to me. She crossed the room and sat at my feet.

"I'm leaving tomorrow." She told me.

"I know. I wish I were going with you."

"You're needed here, Delitha." She looked me straight in the eye. "Right now, life is about your father. Getting him back on his feet. Getting him used to not having someone to care for. He needs to be reminded that there is a world outside his front door. He needs you, Delitha. Stay with him. New York will be there when you're not needed here."

She allowed a few moments of silence. She always knew when to pause.

"I talked with your father. I assumed you had told him of your love for Yosef. I am so terribly sorry. I never meant to break your confidence." She waited for a response, but I had none to give. "There was another matter," she continued, "that I assumed your father had told you. Now that I know he has not, I feel that I must." She adjusted herself, getting more comfortable. "There is property on the outskirts of town. When I was a girl, it was occupied by the Whithrow family. They were a good family, strong marriage, twelve healthy children. The Whithrow family was known for three things, being honest, making babies and being poor."

She took a breath and I took the opportunity to say, "I don't see what this has to do with . . . "

"The Whithrows had a son named Saul," she continued, as if she hadn't heard me. "He had been courting your mother for some time: they had promised themselves to one another. The match made sense." She stopped, cleared her throat. "Saul was determined to have a home of his own before making your mother his wife. He moved on to the next county to work the fields. His intentions were noble. He was to work the fields until he could buy his own plot of land and build her a home worth living in. So, Saul was gone and one day your mother walked into town and on her way back out, my brother, your father, saw her. He had known of her his entire life, from afar obviously; but that day, his eyes were opened to her. Your father was instantly sick with love. He rode his bicycle over to her and asked if he could give her a ride home." She chuckled softly to herself. "Your mother told him, 'I don't ride with boys. However, if you would like to leave your bicycle, you may walk me home.' I hate to describe your mother in this manner, but the truth is, she knew of your father, she knew our family's social standing, our financial status. She recognized the benefits of marrying into the Hancock family versus the Whithrow family. As you can imagine, our father was less than satisfied with his son's choice for a wife, so your grandfather threatened to remove your father from his will. Your father, obviously, chose your mother over his inheritance. It wasn't until after the wedding that he explained the situation to your mother. Once she realized she was neither getting the man she loved, nor the wealth she desired, she fell into a deep depression. Your father thought having children might bring her joy, but as you know, that didn't go as planned either. That's when your father moved out to the country and began preaching. He always had the gift of the Word, but I suppose to him it was one last attempt at bringing her happiness."

"Why would that have brought her happiness?" I asked.

"Perhaps a simpler life. Not that the life of a preacher is simple, but he hoped the community would embrace her and her it. He hoped she would find love in the Lord and that it would be enough to fulfill her. I guess I don't need to tell you that your mother did find love in the Lord, and it did sustain her for quite some time. It was around your third birthday that Saul was taken in an accident at the mill. That is when your mother took to the bottle." She stopped and took my hand. "Perhaps it was out of pity, or perhaps the Lord softened his heart, who knows, but your grandfather called your father into town one afternoon and they made amends. But, by that time your mother was so far into her sin, your father vowed not to waste his inheritance on the drink. He vowed to live by his own means until she was broken of the habit."

"Why are you telling me this?" I asked.

"There are many lessons to be learned from this, Delitha. They will show themselves as you are ready to see them."

I had no response. I turned my back to her. Pulling back the cover, she crawled in bed and wrapped her arms around me. We stayed that way until morning.

Saying goodbye to my Aunt Esther was harder than I could have imagined. It was that day at the station that I felt like I was saying goodbye to my mother. I held on to her until the last call had been made. She walked the length of the passenger car waving at me as the train moved away. I remember standing there all alone, trying my hardest to feel and act like a lady; standing tall and proper, forcing myself to keep the tears for my pillow.

It wasn't until I returned home and stood in the foyer by myself that I felt like anything but a lady. In one split second, my entire childhood came back to me. I stood there and watched myself running up and down the stairs with my hands loaded with linens; darting in and out of the kitchen with full and then empty trays, with sweat bubbling under my nose. I watched as my memory covered every inch of that house in quick little steps, trying hard not to be noticed. And then it happened. She appeared. I gripped my handbag as my childhood self was drug from the kitchen. Drug to the bottom of the staircase. Then I watched with rage as she yelled at me, "Get up there! Now! Before I lock you in the linen closet! Now! Or you'll be sorry! Now! Or else! Now! Or I'll . . ."

I couldn't take it anymore. I remember clutching my bag so hard that I felt my fingernails bend backwards.

"NO!" I yelled at her memory. "YOU CAN'T HURT ME ANYMORE! DO YOU HEAR ME! YOU CAN'T HURT ME ANYMORE!"

I remember raising the bag above my head and turning to the shadow beside me. In all my rage, I saw the shadow as her. It was her shadow hovering over me. With my bag gripped by both hands, I brought it down as hard and fast as I could, screaming with the motion. What I heard next was the sound of glass breaking, then my father's voice.

"Del! What in heaven's name are you doing?"

He was at the top of the stairs. Hanging on to the banister the same way Mother had done the morning Aunt Esther arrived.

"Del! What's gotten into you?"

He rushed down the stairs and gently pulled me from the puddle of shattered glass. It wasn't Mother I had struck, it was our hall tree. I had struck the mirror that hung so beautifully in its wooden frame.

I can't accurately describe what I felt next. In many ways I felt as though something inside of me had given up . . . or rather, given in. There was no use fighting, or fearing, or hating. There was nothing left in that old house to fight or fear or hate. Instead, I suddenly saw the house for what it really was. A house. A house that had been neglected. A house that needed a good cleaning. For the first time, I could see past the dust and brokenness and I could see the beauty and purpose that was hidden underneath.

"I'll clean it up," I told my father. "I'll clean it all up."

I walked past him and down the hall to Mother's cleaning closet. In that small space, I stripped myself of the last dress Aunt Esther had given me and replaced it with an old pair of trousers and work shirt. I wrapped an old towel around my waste, a handkerchief over my hair and stood back to survey the cleaning supplies. Starting with the broken glass, I slowly moved from room to room, wiping away the past as I went. Little did I know that by cleaning that old house, I would be taking my heart on an unexpected journey. A journey that would force me to confront the ghosts from my past; ghosts that hid in the shadows of every room I entered. I entered each room frightened by the memories that lingered there. But, I left each room with a bit more strength and healing having confronted those memories and by wiping them away with the dust and cobwebs.

I had covered every inch of our home. Every inch, with the exception of my father's bedroom. He, and he alone could attempt to air out the memories there. Those memories were not mine to deal with, not mine to confront. So, I left them, knowing that one day my father would take his own journey towards healing and he would come away a stronger man for having dealt with his ghosts himself.

My father had escaped into his bedroom unaware of my cleaning effort. But, I knew he would notice, when his eyes were ready to see it. After sweeping off the front porch I made a fresh glass of lemonade and returned to the porch for fresh air. It was early evening. My back ached and my hands were chapped. I hadn't done such extensive work in years; I had been spoiled in New York. I sat down in one of the rockers my father had made for Mother as an anniversary gift. I had no more than crossed my legs, when one of the supporting boards split and pinched my bottom.

"Ouch!" I called out, jumping to my sore feet. "That wasn't nice," I said to the rocker.

"Talking to chairs is the first sign of insanity."

I quickly turned and found Ida's father coming up our front steps.

"Good evening," he said, tipping his hat.

"Good evening," I said in return. "This isn't what it looks like you know . . ."

"Oh, I know . . ." he laughed. "Rockers can be ornery critters, you don't have to explain a thing to me." He stood smiling.

"It pinched me," I explained, trying to be serious.

He walked over to see for himself.

"You don't look heavy enough to split a plank of wood." He was still smiling.

"Did you need something?" I asked as politely as I could.

"I just came over to visit with your old man."

"He must be sleeping, he hasn't' been out of his room in hours."

"Hmm," was all he said in response. He leaned over for a better look and swiped his hand across the split.

"I helped your father make these."

"You did?"

"Indeed. He didn't get the idea till just a few days before their anniversary. He needed my help to finish them in time."

He examined the rocker as though he were a doctor and it was his patient.

"I can fix this if you'd like," he finally said, still rubbing his hand over the spot. "Wouldn't take much. I could have it back this time tomorrow."

"You don't have to do that . . . really."

He stood tall, towering over me. It was the first time I had considered how broad his chest was. How strong he was.

"Well . . ." I said, thoughtfully.

"There's not much work to be done these days. Let me fix the rocker. In fact, let me spruce them both up for you."

"I'll expect them back this time tomorrow," I said, smiling back at him.

He picked up both rockers, swinging them over his shoulders. I noticed the outline of his muscles through his shirt. Then, I tried not to notice.

22

"The house is sparkling," my father exclaimed as he sat down for breakfast the following morning. "It is so good to have you back." He rubbed his hands together as I stood next to him filling his coffee cup.

"John came by last evening. He was hoping to visit with you."

"Sorry I missed him. John's a good man. He's been a faithful friend."

I stood at the counter and watched him. His eyes were bloodshot and his skin looked thin. He was obviously in some sort of pain.

"What do you have planned for today?" I asked him. "Maybe some country air would do you good . . . we could . . ."

Before I could finish he cleared his throat, "I have some business to take care of today. I'll be having lunch in town. Don't expect me home till dinner."

"Business?" I inquired.

"Yes, nothing too serious." He picked up his coffee and closed his eyes as its warmth slid down his throat.

"Well, what sort of business? Something to do with Mother?"

He sat quietly for a moment, not wanting to answer. Then, finally he forced his head to turn and face me.

"I'm going in to see to Doc Taylor."

"Are you ill?" I asked, taking the seat across from him.

"Not for you to worry, Del."

"Don't leave me out of this," I told him sternly.

"I've had . . ." he hesitated. "I've had headaches. Terrible headaches."

"Is that all?"

"The Doc says it's stress, a lack of sleep . . . all those things I have no control over." He shuffled his feet under the table. "I can't sleep at night, yet I assure you, I could and would like to sleep all day." He rubbed at his temples. "He's going to give me something to help me sleep through the night. Something to help, that's all."

I looked at him; angry at how Mother's death had affected him.

"This too shall pass," he said under his breath, and then he smiled at me and began to fill his plate.

Dear Charlie,

I miss you. Today is the first day I have felt alone here. The house is empty and everything is still. I wish you were here to keep me company. But, I understand that the show must go on. I dream about you. You dance around in my head and bring a smile to my face. Do you miss me, Charlie?

I think of you everyday. Is the show going well? Tell Lizzy hello for me. I miss her too. Don't either of you forget about me. I'll be home soon enough.

All my love,
Maggie

****

"Good as new," John said, as he set the rockers down in their places.

"They look . . . they look perfect," I said, surprised.

He had taken two faded, weathered chairs, and brought back two completely refinished rockers.

"They're beautiful," I said, complimenting his work. "It's like magic."

"Not magic. Just a rag and stain and a few swings of the hammer."

"How can I pay you?" I asked, unable to take my eyes off his work.

"Don't be silly," he said. "I was hoping you would have something else for me to do. It felt good to work with my hands again."

"Follow me," I instructed him, shrugging my shoulders.

I gave him a quick tour of my findings. A post on the staircase, the knob on father's door. The clock in the dining hall that stopped again since I had wound it. The first step down, going out the back door. A cupboard door that wouldn't close all the way. A loose leg that made the kitchen table wobble. I feared my list would overwhelm him. But, he took note of everything that needed work, and he smiled as he followed me through the house and back out to the front porch.

"I've been wanting to come visit Ida again." I told him, "There was just so much around here that I needed to tend to first."

"She understands," he said, with kind eyes. "She left yesterday to stay with her grandma for the week." He took off his hat and ran his hand through his hair. "She and Robert are workin' on their house."

"They'll live in the county then?" I asked, as if I didn't already know.

"Our family belongs in the country." He looked around, "I know this isn't like New York . . . but it might as well be a city. There's nothin' here for a farmer,"

"Why don't you go back?" Then I remembered to whom I was speaking.

"I apologize." I said, putting my head down, embarrassed. "That isn't my business."

John was too kind to let me be embarrassed. "No apology needed." He said, stepping off the porch. "I'll be back tomorrow." He removed his hat and ran his fingers through his hair again. A surge of energy shot through me. My cheeks burned.

There are some feelings we experience on the inside that show themselves on the outside as well. This feeling, whatever it was, stayed with me the remainder of the afternoon and was apparently still noticeable at dinner.

"Del, are you feeling alright? You looked flushed."

"I'm fine, thank you. What did he say?" I prodded, hoping to change the subject.

"Who? Oh, Doc Taylor?"

"Yes, Doc Taylor." I shook my head at him. "I'm worried about you."

"I'm fine." He said. "He gave me something to help me sleep. A few nights of assisted sleep and my body should be back on track." He continued eating as if we were simply discussing the weather.

"What else?"

He looked up at me, annoyed.

"Did he say anything else?"

He set his fork down and straightened up.

"He said I should avoid stress. He suggested getting away for a few days."

"I think that's a great idea. You've been cooped up in this house for far too long."

"Where would I go?"

"Anywhere, go visit Aunt Esther; Lillian would love to cook for you."

"I like your cooking," he said with a smile. "Besides, what would I do in New York? The Doc said relax, not vacation in a busy city."

We both picked at our food.

"No," he said, "I can't leave, you've just arrived. It would be unheard of for me to leave now."

"I'll be here when you get back." He looked surprised. "I've given Ida my word to stay for her wedding."

"You're a good friend," he said letting out a sigh.

"I'm trying to be a good daughter. I want you to pack a bag and go."

He stared at me blankly. "Where?" he asked again.

"Stay at the shack," I told him.

Father had built a shack in the woods behind the church building. He would often retreat there after Sunday fellowship to clear his mind. As a child, I had often daydreamed of faking a bad cough. One bad enough to dismiss me from the Sunday morning service. In my dream, I would tiptoe to the shack and . . . do nothing at all. I would sit alone, worshiping the silence.

"What would I do for food?"

"No one there will let you starve. Knock on one door, let them know where you are staying, and everyone will be bringing you food."

"You're right, you know." He nodded to himself. "And those ladies do know how to cook," he continued, nodding.

"Go," I said again. "I'll be here when you get back."

Father had gone up to pack and I had just finished clearing the table when John knocked on the door.

"Morning," he said, removing his hat as he stepped inside. "Where should I start?"

I looked up the stairs toward my father's room. I knew if he saw John working, he would never leave. He would feel as though he should stay and help.

"How about the clock in the dining hall?"

He nodded and went on his way. I could hear him tinkering around and pulling tools from his satchel. I peeked in on him once or twice and was on my way for a third look when my father came down the hall.

"You're sure about this?" he asked one more time.

"Go and don't come back till you're ready," I told him.

He took my face in his free hand and kissed my cheek.

"Wait," I ran into the kitchen and returned with a small box.

"It's just some bread and fruit. In case you get hungry on the way."

"I'll be taking the car. Are you sure you'll be alright?"

"I have nowhere to go. If I need anything, I'll go next door."

The instant Father stepped off the porch, John came out into the hallway.

"Could I trouble you for an old rag?" His voice was loud and startled me. "It's the one thing I forgot to bring along."

I led him to the cleaning closet.

"You should be able to find just about anything in here."

He stepped inside, having to duck through the small door.

"Your mother kept an orderly home," he said once inside. "Even her cleaning closet is organized."

I let out a nervous laugh. I suppose it was Mother's desire to have an organized cleaning closet, but it was my hands that spent so many hours perfecting her vision.

John spent the morning working on our clock. I moved around the house listening to his work. Every so often a small clinking sound would come from the room. Then a clanking sound would follow. I was curious as to the inward parts of the machine. Had it been my father in the dining hall, I would have enjoyed standing over his shoulder, handing him tiny tools as he asked for them. But, this was not my father.

I found myself embarrassed at the memories of running in the Sundays' field and spying as Ida's father worked the ground. I blushed at the thought of him being in the next room as Ida and I bathed together. "We were children," I reminded myself. But, I was embarrassed nonetheless. I found myself regretting the childish games Ida and I would play in his presence. Regretting having ever danced in his living room as he played his guitar. I regretted having ever been a child before his eyes. "Don't be silly," I told myself. But, I couldn't help it. There was something in me that wanted to make sure he saw me as a lady. Not the child he once knew.

When the clock was back up and running, John said there was rain coming, that he should tackle the back step while it was still dry out. I found myself pacing the house, not wanting to be busy when he finally came back in. I found myself waiting for him. Then I felt embarrassed and didn't want to seem as though I were waiting on him. I wanted to look busy, but not be busy. There was nothing on the first floor to be done, nothing I could pretend to be doing. I made my way upstairs and had just stepped in my bedroom when I heard his voice.

"All done."

He stood at the bottom of the stairs smiling, shaking his head.

"What?" I asked.

"You look like your mother."

I felt my face tighten.

"You look the way your mother looked when she was your age."

Still, I said nothing.

"She was beautiful," He added.

My face remained tight and my eyebrows fought my rigid brow to rise above their resting place. Suddenly I felt a pit in my stomach, an ache that took me by surprise. A tingling sensation ran through my body.

"Are you hungry?"

"Pardon?"

"It's past lunch time. You've been working hard. Are you hungry?" I stammered over my words and began to blush as he set down his toolbox and examined his hands.

"I'm a mess. You don't want me in your kitchen like this."

"Go home and wash up," I told him. "If you aren't going to let me pay you, at least let me feed you." I found myself smiling. "Lunch will be served in fifteen minutes." At last my face and my words seemed to be at ease.

Our conversation was light, as was the meal. We both seemed to feel a bit uncomfortable at first. This was the first time I felt we were equals. That I, too, was an adult. We sat silent for some time, searching for common ground. Something to talk about.

"What did you miss most?" he finally asked. "While you were in New York, I mean. What did you miss most about home?"

I thought for a moment. What had I missed? There had to be something.

"What's the first thing that came to mind?" he asked.

"Trees," I said, straightening my back.

"Trees?"

"Yes. Trees. There aren't enough trees in the city."

He frowned and let out a "huh" sound.

"What do you miss about home?" I asked in return. "I'm sorry, that isn't my business," I added quickly.

"Now, the way I see it, Delitha," he sat up straight and folded his hands, "We're both adults. And for now we're neighbors; you can ask me any question that I feel comfortable asking you." He picked up his fork again.

"Alright then," I said, taking a deep breath. "What do you miss about home?"

"The trees," he answered.

We exchanged a grin.

"There are trees here, I know. But, these are not my trees. I miss my land."

"Why don't you go back?" I asked, reluctantly.

"It isn't time yet," he answered. "You know, we don't always feel at home where the Good Lord puts us. It was clear to me that we should come here. But, it hasn't been made clear that it's time to leave. Is it clear that you should return to New York?"

"I had to come home," I told him. "It was the right thing to do."

He nodded in agreement.

"I am expected to return," I finally told him.

"So, it's clear to you then?" he asked.

"Nothing is clear to me," I confessed.

23

John had been right. The following morning we were greeted by a heavy rainfall. I was standing on the front porch sticking my hand out into the wetness when John came through the gate. He wore a long trench coat, holding his toolbox in one hand and an umbrella in the other.

"I remember when you and Ida would stand outside for hours trying to catch the rain. It seems like all you managed to catch was a cold."

"Perhaps my luck will be better today," I said, surprised that I was no longer embarrassed by his recollection of my childhood.

"Perhaps," he said, shaking off his umbrella. He removed his coat and draped it over the back of the nearest rocker.

"What's first on your list today?"

"Let's see . . ." I wasn't sure why I hesitated, I knew exactly what I wanted done. "If you don't mind, you could start upstairs. The door to father's room doesn't latch. The knob is broken."

"On my way," he said, letting himself in the front door.

I stayed on the porch catching handfuls of water and splashing it on my face. Just as Ida and I had done so many years before.

By noon, John had fixed the doorknob and the cupboard in the kitchen. Once again I provided a meal as my way of saying thank you.

"So," he started, "When you were in New York, you missed the trees. Now that you are here, what do you miss about New York?"

"I miss Aunt Esther and Lillian," I told him, without hesitation. Then I wiggled in my seat surprised that my first thought was not of Charlie.

"Who's Lillian?" he asked, genuinely interested.

"Oh, well, Lillian is Aunt Esther's . . . well, I suppose she is Aunt Esther's maid."

He looked confused.

"Well, I know Lillian is her maid, but I never gave it much thought. They acted more like best friends. They're just two lonely women who live together.

One of them provides the money and the other provides the meals."

I laughed to myself as I described them. "They are both dear friends, I'm thankful to have spent so much time with them."

"Hmm . . . you know we never thought you would be gone so long. Ida had a real hard time at first. She cried for you almost everyday."

"She did?" I asked, surprised.

"She did. Carolyn and I had to remind her to live. But, I think after that first year went by, she realized she had to stop waiting for you. She realized she had to move on."

We both sat silent and sad.

"She's trying not to get attached to you again," he finally said. "She knows you'll be going back. She doesn't want to get close and then lose you again."

The truth was, and we both knew it, even if I stayed things would never be as they were. Too much time had passed, too many people had come between us, giving us enough experiences that we couldn't possibly share them all with one another. We had been separated during the years that molded us into women. Our friendship could certainly start anew, but it would never be as it was. And, to my surprise, I didn't find myself longing for Ida and her friendship. Although I would never have admitted it, I felt a sense of relief that she was not next door and that she was not calling wanting to "get together" for old time's sake. I had moved on.

The following day, John appeared at my front door right on time, ready to finish off my list of chores.

"All that's left," I told him, "is the leg on the kitchen table."

"I didn't notice it being wobbly," he said, following me into the kitchen.

"That is because," I knelt down and pulled a folded newspaper out from under the leg, "of this." I held up the paper with one hand and leaned on the table with the other. The jolt of my weight was enough to send the table and me off balance.

John laughed, "Ah, the newspaper trick."

I watched as he measured the leg and scribbled down the numbers.

"Well," he said under his breath, "I think . . . instead of replacing the entire leg, I may just saw this one off, add a block of wood at the top. You'll never know it had a problem."

He gathered a few select items from his box and said, "I'll be back shortly." I had begun preparations for lunch when he returned.

"I'll need to turn the table over," he said as he entered the kitchen.

With one hand he reached under the side and tipped the table. He grabbed two of the good legs and set the table down on its top.

"Maybe you'd rather I do this outside. It'll make a bit of a mess." He was kneeling and looking up at me. His eyes were twinkling.

"No," I told him quickly. "I would enjoy watching. Besides, this room needs a good sweeping anyway."

It wasn't long before the table was put back together, the floor had been swept, and we were seated enjoying an early lunch.

"There must be something more I can do for you," I told him. "You've done so much . . . I don't feel like this is enough."

"There is one thing," he said quietly, after thinking for a moment. "Ida wants to wear her mother's dress for her wedding. It needs to be sewn in a few places and it needs a good cleaning . . ."

"I would love to," I said, before he could finish.

I asked John if I might get started on Ida's dress that very afternoon. He obliged, and I returned home with him after lunch. In a matter of days, John had gone from my dear friend's father, to a dear friend. I felt as though we both looked forward to his daily visit. And we both seemed a bit disappointed when the work was done. I was pleased to be of some assistance to him, and he seemed pleased to have me in his home.

"Please sit down," he said, offering me my choice of seats. "I'm a grandfather, you know." He had stepped into the kitchen and brought back a photo of Jack and Laura along with a glass of juice, which he sat on the table before me. In the picture, Jack and Laura stood beside a large oak tree; Jack's hand rested on the head of a golden retriever. Laura held a baby in her arms and three more pressed against her legs.

"They're a beautiful family," I said, handing him back the photo.

"Luke and Virginia have a few themselves. I've never seen them though."

"Never?" I asked, surprised.

"When you have as many children as we did, you're bound to have at least one that leaves and never looks back. Luke's the one."

I was surprised, and not.

"What about you? When do you plan on settling down?"

I looked down at my hands folded in my lap. My skin felt hot.

"It isn't all my planning," I said with a grin. "There has to be a man involved in there too, you know."

This was a topic I had never discussed with a man. Suddenly, my heart began to race. I filled my mouth with juice and held it there before swallowing, wishing it were liquor. Then I cursed myself for entertaining the thought.

"You have a beautiful home," I managed to say. "I would love to see the rest of it."

"Well, may I show you around?" He offered his arm. I stood and accepted his offer. But, something changed in that moment. In that brief conversation. It was his question, "When do you plan on settling down?" My mind went back to my sixteenth birthday, when I opened the box assuming there was a ring inside, only to find a theater ticket staring back at me. Then, more recently, my eighteenth birthday, when I did receive a ring, but there was no proposal to go with it. My head felt fuzzy and I stopped for a moment to catch my breath.

"Is something the matter?" he asked, looking down at me.

"No . . . I'm quite alright. Thank you."

I closed my eyes for a brief moment and then allowed him to lead me around his home. Every room in the house was grander than the last. My expectations of this home were more than met. Each room was adorned in the richest shades of green, maroon, gold, and royal blue. It was lovely, elegant. We moved slowly, hesitating in the center of each room, as though touring an art exhibit. He would pause to explain the history behind a certain heirloom or to show off what new items would be handed down as heirlooms. The home was brilliant. There were eight rooms on the second floor. Though unoccupied, each room was completely furnished. The master suite was the only room I did not enter. John closed the door as we passed by. That simple act impressed me, flattered me. John pressed upon me a level of respect that Charlie never knew I deserved. Not just myself, but any woman. John pressed upon me a feeling I couldn't explain; one I hadn't expected to feel, at least not here, in Georgia.

At the end of the hall stood a small table that held three items. All of which were beautiful in their own way. The first item to catch my eye was a tall, green oil lamp. It wore an Aladdin hat upon its head, which sparkled with the light that shone through the window directly behind it. Sitting below and to the side of the lamp was the Sunday family Bible. Its once brown, now-black binding was starting to tear. In the corner of the table, sitting upon a tea-stained doily, was a photograph of Carolyn. She held her eyes closed as she sniffed the bouquet she held in her hands. I recognized the dress she wore from Luke's wedding.

"What do you miss most about her?" I asked quietly.

He smiled at me, thankful for the opportunity to bring a memory to mind.

"You'd be surprised. I thought I would miss her scent, her voice, or her smile. But, those aren't the things I find myself missing." He put his hand on the small of my back and led me back down the hall. He left his hand there as we descended the stairs. "For instance, today," he continued "your presence has reminded me that I miss the company of an honest woman." I looked at him inquisitively. "When an honest woman enters a room, she is followed by a sweetness that calms a man's soul."

"I must admit," I said in too loud a voice, "I am impressed. Did Carolyn see to the decorations?"

"She did. We never had the means to make our home look like this. This was her dream. I thank God every day she was able to live among such nice things, even if it were only for a short time."

"If you don't mind my asking . . ."

He knew my question before I asked it. "Your father gave us this home. Along with the means to make it our own and maintain it."

For a moment I strained to hear him. Surely I had misunderstood.

"I don't mean to sound as though I don't believe you, but *my* father?"

He smiled at me and chuckled to himself.

"What you're really thinking is why am I still here. Just me in this big old house."

"No," I thought to myself . . . that was not what I was really thinking.

"I've tried to give this house back more times than I can count. Your father just shakes his head and says I'm not done with it yet. He says I fulfilled one purpose but that there is one more yet to be fulfilled."

"I don't mean to be rude," I said, straightening my dress. "But, what exactly was the first purpose?"

"Your mother needed a companion."

"I don't understand. Ida explained in her letter that you moved here for Albert, for better schooling, better opportunities."

"The fact that your father gave us this house is between your father and me. It didn't seem necessary to explain it to Ida or anyone else."

"I see. What were you saying about Mother?"

"Your father had exhausted all his options. Your mother's end seemed inevitable. She was asking for Carolyn, but we couldn't come as often as she needed. Your father offered us this home, more as a gift for your mother than to us. But, it was a great benefit to us all."

"She asked for Carolyn?"

"I suppose it worked when you think about it. Your mother hung on for quite some time. They would sit from sun up, to sun down laughing and sharing thoughts on life. On death."

I felt the blood drain from my face, perhaps from my entire body. I slithered to a chair by the window; I lowered myself and hung my head.

She had asked for Carolyn, not for me. Why was I so shocked by this? Really, why would Mother have asked for me?

"What do you miss most about your mother?" He asked, solemnly. I raised my head, crossed my feet at the ankles, and cleared my throat.

"Peace, relaxation, confidence, pride, silence. These are all the things I would miss if she were to come back."

He turned quickly to meet my gaze. Clearly he was neither enlightened nor amused by my answer.

"It takes time, Delitha. Remember what I said about . . ."

"Your wife and my mother were two very different people," I said, cutting him off. He moved toward me and knelt at my feet. I felt my teeth clenching inside my jaws.

"They were very different," he agreed. "In fact, sometimes I didn't understand how the two of them became such close friends. But, they were both sinners, as are we all." He spoke slowly and softly, yet his words stung my face and pounded like boulders inside my head. I rose from my seat and stormed out into the hallway.

"Don't talk to me of sin. Don't talk to me of my mother!"

He followed me, finally catching me as I reached the front door. Taking me by the arm, he stopped and spun me around.

"It's not yourself you're running from, Delitha. It's your past."

"You don't know!" I snapped.

"I know what destroyed your mother! Don't let the memory of that destroy you, too!"

I turned to run, but he wouldn't let me. He drew me into him. My head went to his chest and his arms held me there. He held me there until the tears had come and gone, till our bodies had created uncomfortable warmth. Until I felt as though it were God himself embracing me. At last he loosened his grip and I leaned back against the wall, my eyes closed.

I remember being overtaken by a strange sensation. I went in to his arms feeling like a child, being comforted by a father figure. But, when he released me, I felt like a woman, being held by a man.

"Forgive me," I said softly, opening my eyes.

"There is nothing to forgive." He wiped a tear from my cheek.

I sniffed and smiled, trying to act as though nothing had happened. As though I had kept my emotions to myself.

"Where is this wedding dress that needs fixing?" I raised my eyebrows as I spoke, trying hard to erase my fit from his memory.

"It can wait," he said, sympathetically.

"No . . . now, I said I would do it today, and I will."

He brought his hand to my face one more time to wipe away the last tear.

24

John led me up into the attic and opened a large trunk that was covered in dust and cobwebs. I took the dress into my arms and pressed it against my own body. I wondered if this day would ever come for me. Would I ever open a small box and find more than theater tickets staring back at me? Would I ever have more than the ring that was beginning to feel too tight on my finger?

John set me up at Carolyn's old sewing table and I began stitching and repairing the damage that time had done. John had long since disappeared, and I sat alone working to the sounds of the birds outside. They sang sweet songs to me as I imagined Ida wrapped up like a gift in this beautiful white dress. Ida . . . she had surprised me in so many ways. The way she looked at me at Mother's burial. The way she touched my hair and stared as if I were a circus sideshow. I was still shocked that Ida never told me of her mother's pregnancy and the cause of her death. She had failed to mention the seriousness of her relationship with Robert. There had been no exchange of giggles over their romance. She had changed. She had turned into a lady during my absence, just as she had feared I would do. We had both changed. We had grown up and apart. There was a small part of me that wanted to let her in. Let her in to this new life of mine. But, could she, would she, understand my relationship with Yosef? How we had recreated ourselves? Could she ever see me as who I had become, the one and only Maggie Fairchild?

"Ouch" I called aloud, rushing my finger into my mouth. While lost in my thoughts, I had led the needle into my fingertip. The skin around the puncture pulsed with my heart. The blood was warm on my tongue. It tasted salty. I envisioned Mother and immediately turned my head to the side and spit the blood from my mouth. Mother. There was no escaping her. Even as she lay in the ground, her memory taunted me as if she were still lingering in the house next door.

"Will you ever leave me be?" I jumped to my feet and turned to the window behind me. I had a perfect view of Father's house. It looked old, weathered. As if no one had lived there for years. That's when it struck me. No one had lived there for years. The only life that house held had left and moved on. My parents had merely existed in that house. They had not lived. Suddenly I felt sadness. As strange as it sounds, I felt sadness for the house. I could hear John quoting my father, "Every house has a purpose" he had said. What was the purpose of our house? Would it ever thrive? Would it ever be allowed to bounce around the sound of laughter and proudly protect a loving family? It was then that I looked down at Ida's dress. It was balled up in my hands. There was a tiny spot of blood that had left my finger and soaked into the white fabric.

It took some time, but I was finally able to remove the blood before a stain set in. I hung the dress out back to dry and soak up the smell of the sun. It was so warm that day. I closed my eyes and lifted my face to the sky. My body had finally begun to relax when I smelled it. Something was burning.

"John! Is everything alright?" I followed the smell into the kitchen and found John leaning over the stove.

He turned to me when I entered the room and he looked embarrassed.

"I was trying to make you a meal for a change . . . but, I think I've ruined it."

I rushed to his side, grabbing Carolyn's apron as I went. Wrapping it around my waist I nudged him to the side.

"Let me see what you've done," I pulled the skillet off the stove. Without my asking, John sat a hot pad on the table, and I placed the skillet there.

"Fried chicken . . . you made fried chicken?"

"I told you I can cook . . . I just lost track of time with this one."

He went back to the stove, "Everything else looks good."

And it was good, even the burnt chicken. We spent the meal laughing and reminiscing and speculating on how long my father would stay away.

"He needs time," John advised me. "Just give him space . . . he'll be back to normal soon enough."

"I don't know what normal is for him," I admitted. "I've been gone too long. Maybe I should have stayed."

"No," he said. "Think how different you would be if you had stayed. You would be a tired, bitter woman by now. Instead, you are a beautiful, vibrant, young lady with energy to spare."

"Ok, with all that flattery there must be something else you want . . ."

We began laughing and exchanging words that could have been mistaken for flirting. We picked at one another while we moved around the kitchen, clearing the table. I washed the dishes and he stood next to me drying them and putting them away. I was drying my hands on the apron when the kitchen door swung open, surprising us both.

"Ida!" John exclaimed. "What a surprise!"

She stood still, looking from one of us to the other.

"You're getting it wet," she finally said to me.

"What . . . I'm getting what wet . . . ?"

John looked to be just as confused as I was. Ida marched toward me and pulled the apron from my waist.

"You're getting it wet," she said again.

She brushed the apron off and hung it back on the nail by the door. I noticed John put his head down and closed his eyes for a moment.

"This is not yours," Ida said to me, still looking at the apron.

"Ida . . ." I began, "I didn't mean any harm. "

"Why are you in my momma's kitchen?" She marched toward me again.

John stepped in between us. "I invited her. She was helping clean up. I let her wear the apron."

"Well, you shouldn't have," she said in a loud voice. "It isn't hers. It's momma's."

She turned and stormed from the kitchen. We heard her stomping up the stairs and once in her bedroom, we heard her door slam shut.

"I'm sorry," John said, placing his hands on my shoulders. "I didn't know . . . "

"I'll talk with her," I said, stepping away from him.

"Maybe it would be best if I . . ."

"No," I interrupted, "she and I need to talk."

I followed Ida to her room and calmly called her name as I tapped on her door. I had expected a childish response of "go away" . . . but that wasn't what I got. She opened the door and faced me.

"Why are you here?" she asked, boldly.

"I was mending your wedding gown; John made me dinner in return."

"John? Now you're calling my father John?"

She turned and crossed the room, flopping herself face down on her bed. I closed the door behind me and joined her.

"Ida, you know I would never hurt you on purpose. I didn't know my being here would upset you."

She sat up and wiped her hair from her face. "I didn't know it would either." She looked down at the bed, unable to make eye contact. "You called him John."

"Ida . . ." I didn't understand why this was affecting her so. "All I can say is I'm sorry."

She stood and paced the room. "You mended my gown?"

"Yes. I hope that's alright with you."

She forced a grin.

"Yes, good timing actually. I came home early because we've moved up the wedding date." She walked over to the window and stuck her head out for air. "Robert's grandpa is dying. Waiting two more weeks might be too late." She spoke quickly and involuntarily touched her stomach as she spoke. "We're getting married after the service on Sunday."

"That soon," was all I could say.

"I spoke with your father. He's agreed to marry us. I came back for the dress and a few little things. And to talk with . . ." She stopped and looked at me. "I don't like you calling him John."

Ida and her father left the next morning. My father returned home for his best suit and we drove together for the Sunday service. I remember my father taking a stroll through the cemetery before he came inside. He had brought a bundle of flowers that I had assumed were for the wedding, but I was wrong; he gently laid them on Mother's headstone. He knelt there for a moment. Then met me at the door.

"I'm going to deliver the message today."

"You are?" I asked in surprise. My father had not stood at the pulpit since before I left for New York.

"Well, then," I said, trying to sound supportive. "I'll see you after the service." He gave me a gentle half hug and walked down the aisle, shaking hands as he went. I watched and listened. "Morning, Brother Hancock." I heard one man say as he stood to shake my father's hand.

With each handshake, he began to stand a little taller and hold his chin a little higher. This was where he belonged. He was a messenger. Perhaps this was where he needed to be. What he needed to heal.

My father stood before his flock and waited, giving everyone a moment to find their seats. I was one of the last ones to do so. I went slowly, watching everyone, as everyone watched me. As I walked down the aisle to my seat, I found images from my past dancing before me.

Ida was sitting with her legs crossed at the ankle, her hair in pigtails. She was no more than seven years old. She grinned and pointed to her loose tooth as I took my seat. Albert sat next to her. He was fiddling with two sticks he had sneaked in. He stuck his tongue out at me as I sat down.

Simon ignored me, as usual. He sat flipping through his Bible, pretending to be interested. Then there was Luke. He looked angry. Or perhaps disappointed. In what, none of us would ever know. Jack sat up straight in his seat. He was licking the palm of his hand and then rubbing the wetness on the back of his hair. Carolyn was next. She was beautiful. Her hair was pinned up and two small flowers were sticking out the back. Ida had no doubt put them there. Carolyn smiled when our eyes met. She had always loved me as if I were one of her own. Then there was John. He sat looking straight ahead, gripping his Bible. His face was tan from the fields. Although he was a large man, everything about him seemed gentle.

I closed my eyes a moment, and when I opened them, the Sunday family began disappearing one by one. Jack, then Luke, then Simon, then Albert, then Carolyn. I looked to the back of the chapel and Ida was sitting with those, whom after that day, would be her new family. She was whispering to Robert. As I turned toward my seat, I realized that John was the only one left. He was sitting alone, facing the front, gripping his Bible, his hair a handsome salt and pepper. He turned and smiled when he saw me.

That morning my father spoke of love. "How amazing it is," he said, "to be loved by someone who would put down his life for you." I am certain that everyone in the room envisioned the son of God hanging on the cross. Putting His life down for each of us. But that isn't what came to my mind. Instead, I saw my father putting down everything he held dear to sit by

Mother's side while she wasted away. She lost her life. But, in many ways, he lost his, too.

My mind was swimming with thoughts of my father, thoughts of Ida, thoughts of Jesus hanging on the cross, thoughts of Mother lying in the ground. It took a nudge to my knee to bring my thoughts back to the present. John had crossed his legs, and in the process he had nudged my knee with his. It was an accidental contact. An accident, nonetheless, that sent a surge of energy and warmth over me. My head quickly turned in his direction. He was still looking straight ahead; unaware of what he had done to me.

25

Ida and Robert were married under the same old oak tree that had shaded Luke and Virginia on their wedding day. My father stopped only once to pull his handkerchief from his pocket and wipe at his eyes. He embraced them both at the close of the ceremony and presented them to the crowd as husband and wife.

The ladies of the congregation had covered three tables with food and drink. The men had taken their seats and began tuning their guitars, fiddles, and harmonicas. Ida and Robert danced for a song or two, and then John cut in. He took his daughter in his arms and instead of dancing, he simply held her. Everyone stopped what they were doing, the music even stopped before the song had ended. Everything. Everything stopped to witness the overwhelming love between a father and his little girl. I sat beneath that old tree and took it all in. A breeze came through and tossed my hair. My father winked at me from where he stood. "What sweetness," I could hear Aunt Esther saying. "What sweetness."

John led his daughter back into the arms of her new husband, and the music began again. I sat, watching him walk toward me with his long, steady stride.

"Would you care to dance?" he asked.

"Oh, you don't want to dance with me. . ." I began. But he didn't let me finish. Instead he held out his hand and simply said, "Yes, I do."

John placed his free hand on my hip and I placed mine on his shoulder. We began moving to the music and before we had taken more than two steps I found myself laughing aloud.

"Am I that bad of a dancer?" he asked, stepping back from me.

"No!" I assured him. "I was just reminded of the first time I went dancing in New York. I went with . . . a friend of mine." I laughed again. "They dance quiet differently in New York." We exchanged a smile, "Forgive me. I wasn't poking fun at you."

"I'd like to hear more about New York. That's somewhere I've never been."

"Oh, there's not much to tell." I lied.

"Ida kept wondering when you would write to tell her of a beau. She was surprised when that letter never came."

I felt myself looking around, suddenly aware that we were dancing before an audience. I caught sight of my father smiling at us.

"I . . . uh . . . well I . . . I did have a beau." I cleared my throat.

Before he could respond, the music stopped and we all stepped away from our partners to applaud.

To my surprise, John never again inquired about the beau I had mentioned. Perhaps he was being a gentleman, or perhaps he had no interest. I found myself shocked at the fact that I cared. I found my way to the refreshments and had just picked up a glass of iced tea when I felt a hand on my back.

"I'm so glad you stayed," Ida said to me.

We hugged and she took the tea from my hand and set it back on the table.

"Would you walk with me?" she asked.

There were many things about Ida and I both that had changed over the years. But, there were some things we could still see in one another. We walked past the chapel and down the path to the pond. Ida stopped at the edge of the water and began unzipping her dress.

"Ida!" I exclaimed, "this is your wedding day!"

"Ah, the party's not going anywhere. Come on."

In a split second she was down to her slip and in the water.

"Race ya," she called, pointing to the dock.

Without thinking, I stripped off my own dress and met her in the chilly water. Even without her head start, she would have out swam me. She was always faster than I was.

The dock was still floating in the center of the pond. The boards were beginning to rot in certain places, but it was still steady and served its purpose.

"I knew you wouldn't be an old spinster," I told her as I climbed up and fell to my knees beside her. We were both panting for air and we spread out on our backs, closing our eyes in the sunshine.

"It makes sense, you know." She turned her head trying to look at me through squinted eyes.

"What?"

"You and my father."

I didn't respond. A strange sensation shot through my body.

"I admit it's a little strange . . . disgusting even," she smiled. "I mean, it is my father, after all. I'll never sit and exchange bedroom advice with you."

"Ida!" I yelled, slapping her side with my nearest arm.

She began laughing. "Well, I won't . . . I don't want to hear about that. Promise me."

"Ida . . . I swear, I haven't the slightest idea what you're talking about."

I turned my head the other way and fought to catch my breath. Ida sat up, letting her hair down to ring out the water.

"It's so obvious," she said. "When I saw you in my mother's apron . . . it was so obvious, it made me angry."

"Ida . . ."

"Let me finish," she snapped. "This is hard for me, but I need to say it." Her voice cracked. "I love my father, and I love you. If the two of you are happy together then so be it. Who am I to stand in your way?"

"Ida, I have no reason to think your father . . ."

"He does," she interrupted. "I can see it in his eyes."

Monday's morning light met me with as many changes as that autumn breeze so many years ago. I opened my eyes, expecting to be alone; I instead found my father placing a tray on my nightstand.

"Rise and shine!" he sang aloud as our eyes met. He crossed the room and threw back my curtains, allowing the morning glory to burn my eyes. Turning my head away from the light, I noticed the contents on that breakfast tray. An omelet lay curled on its side. As if trying to stay warm, two sausage links huddled next to it. There were thin apple slices, sprinkled with cinnamon, arranged in a half moon on the edge of the plate. Father's liquid dirt was nowhere to be found. In its place sat a large glass of freshly squeezed orange juice.

"Breakfast in bed? What did I do to deserve this?"

"Nothing," he replied, "Isn't that the beauty of it?" I felt certain a short sermon would follow and I almost regretted having asked the question when he darted for the door. "You take your time. Eat slowly. Enjoy it. When you're dressed, come down to my office, I have something for you." He smiled and quickly shut the door behind him.

The breakfast father prepared was, to my surprise, very good. There was not a crumb left on my plate as I stood and stretched my body. My back let out a series of pops as my arms attempted to reach higher than the morning before. I dressed slowly, enjoying the fullness of my belly, the light streaming across my floor. I could hear my father down the stairs humming to himself.

Father was sitting at his desk, still humming, as he rummaged through his desk drawers. His cheeks were rosy, his eyes dancing. "Ah, you're here. Wonderful." He waved his hand at me. "Come in, come in. Sit down." I felt as though I were in the company of a stranger. "Sit, sit. Scoot closer, come here." He spoke quickly, excitedly. "Last night, I had the strangest dream. Your mother was standing over me telling me to get out of bed." He rested both arms on the desk and leaned forward as he spoke. "She led me to her wardrobe where she pulled out a small box. Inside were two letters, one addressed to you and one to me." He took a deep breath and smiled, exposing all his teeth.

"That is a strange dream," I told him. "Perhaps you should stop drinking all that coffee before you sleep."

"No, no . . . it wasn't the coffee. Let me finish." He rose, still leaning into me as he pressed both palms against the desk. "This morning when I woke, I had this strange feeling that I should check the wardrobe, and you won't believe what I found."

"A box? Full of mother's old letters?"

"Yes!" he exclaimed.

"That box has been there for years. Letters from Carolyn and . . ."

He pulled his hands from the desk sending papers flying in every direction.

"No, there was more than that. Del, there were two letters resting on top, tied together with ribbon. One addressed to you and one to me."

He stared, waiting for a reaction.

"I . . . I don't know what to say. Did you open them?"

"No, not yet. I wanted you to be here. I wanted us to read them together."

"I'm not sure that . . ."

He shoved the letter at me before I could finish.

"Go ahead, I'll even let you go first. Read it aloud."

I stood, unable to take my eyes off my name. Delitha, written in a script that was Mother's alone. Moving to the door, I looked up to find my father, eyes closed, smelling his envelope. "If it's all the same to you," I whispered, "I think I'd rather be alone to read this." He hesitated, then quickly sat and reached for his letter opener.

I moved to the porch, then to the kitchen, then to my room again. I couldn't bring myself to open it. Wasn't sure I wanted to see what she had to say. Couldn't find a safe, comfortable place. Then it hit me, and I raced down the stairs and out the door. I could only read this letter in one place.

I had unintentionally ignored Ol' Willy since I returned. He, like the rest of us, seemed older. His bark seemed thicker, yet it was breaking away from the trunk. Though his branches hung in a tired manner, they still seemed to tighten around me as I crawled beneath them. "Hello, old friend," I said, stroking his trunk. "It's been too long. The years have been good to you," I chuckled under my breath. "Isn't that what I'm suppose to say?" I took a series of deep breaths and slowly tore open the envelope that was now moist from my sweating hands. "What do you think she has to say?" The wind blew ever so slightly, allowing a branch to touch my back. "Well, there is only one way to find out."

Upon opening her letter, I found that the writing, unlike that on the envelope, was not Mother's. In my mind, I pictured Carolyn sitting next to her bed, slowly writing as Mother composed her letter out loud. It made the letter seem impersonal, as though it were a message from someone else's mother. Yet, as I read the words, I began to find my mother. She was there, in the message. Not the mother I knew when I left with Aunt Esther, nor was it the mother I lived with in this house, it was the mother I remembered in my heart rather than in my mind. It was the mother that cradled and sang lullabies to me as a baby. It was the mother in the photograph that fell to the earth as I separated the pages of the letter.

In the photograph, she was sitting on the front porch in a white rocker. Her hair was down, resting on her shoulders. There was a Mason jar full of flowers sitting next to her on a small wooden table; a half-empty glass of lemonade sat at her feet, along with a blanket and a stack of wooden blocks my diddy had made for me. I was standing on her lap. She gripped me at the waist as we pressed our cheeks together. Her smile was brilliant. A small bubble glistened on my chin. She was glowing with motherhood. That was the mother I found in this letter. The mother I wanted back so badly.

To my daughter, Delitha,

If you are reading this, the Good Lord has taken me home. A home where I am no longer hurting or wanting for anything.

It's amazing what goes through one's mind while staring death in the face. I have dreamed about you and the young lady you have become. I have dreamed of the years I have missed. Not just the years while you were away, but also the years we spent together in this very house. I have not been the mother you needed, or deserved. The fact that I can only admit this to you after I'm gone is proof of that.

There are few things in this world I know to be true, true beyond all doubt. I know I did not deserve you or your father and I know I do not deserve the restful peace that will come with my last breath.

Delitha, please don't allow my shortcomings to keep you from what is right. Live the life you were intended to live. Do you remember that day at the pond when you told me you hated me? That was so long ago. I want you to know that I don't blame you for that. If I had had the nerve to say anything back to you that day, it would have simply been that I hated me too. I'm sorry you hated me. I'm sorry. When we meet again, we will have been made right, I only hope you will recognize me.

Please forgive me, and know that I have so much love for you. So much love that the thought of it frightens me. Till we meet again, my dear.

Your Mother

Never before had I clung so tightly to a piece of paper. Never before had I cried so hard; so freely. I rested my head on the trunk of the tree and felt the spirit of my mother embrace me.

When there were no more tears to be formed in my eyes, I rose and made my way to John's front door, still clenching the letter and photograph.

One, two, three knocks and still no answer, yet the door was not latched. There was an unfamiliar sound coming from inside. My feet stepped as lightly as possible as I followed the sound from the foyer to the entrance of the kitchen. With my treasures in one hand, the other gently pushed on the door, and that is where I found him. He was sitting at the table hunched over with his face buried in his arms. The sound, it was more than crying, more than weeping. He was mourning. For on the table, setting before him, was a framed picture of Carolyn. She smiled at him with tender eyes. His body shook and swayed like a large log bobbing in unsteady waters. He wasn't ready. He hadn't said good-bye to her. I tiptoed out of the house, giving him the privacy I would have wanted.

My father was coming from the kitchen with two cups of coffee when I entered the foyer. His eyes were swollen and bloodshot, yet there was no sign of his heavy heart. "You have a visitor," he said to me. "Quite unexpected, I might add." I turned the corner into his study to find Charlie leaning against the wall, lighting a cigarette.

"Maggie! My dear, come to me!"

He crossed the room and took me in his arms.

"You don't mind that I've given your little girl a pet name, do you?" He flashed my father his trained smile. My father didn't answer.

"What are you doing here?" I asked, filling the awkward silence. "When did you arrive?"

"I arrived just a few moments ago. My God, look at you." He held me at arm's length. "You look as though you haven't slept a wink since you've been here. Let me take you home." He patted his breast pocket with pride.

"I have the tickets right here. We'll be taking the afternoon train." He looked from me to my father and back again. "Let's freshen up, shall we?" He took my hand and nodded to my father. "We'll be down shortly." He took a few steps and turned to me when I did not follow, "Maggie, come."

It might as well have been my mother pulling me up those stairs. Pulling me in a direction I did not want to go, yet pulling me with such strength, I hadn't the nerve to fight against it. I closed my eyes and became that little girl whose feet couldn't keep up. I slipped to my knees, just long enough to slow her down. Slow him down. Slow down whoever it was tugging at my arm.

When we reached the bedroom, my hand was red and my knees burned.

"Look at you. What have they done with you?"

"What?"

"Just look at you, you're a fright!" He stood before me, his hands on his hips. "Where should we start? Where are your bags?"

"My bags?"

"Your bags, Maggie. Where are your bags?"

"I shared a trunk with Aunt Esther."

"How on earth did you plan on coming home?" he asked impatiently.

"I hadn't planned on staying," I explained.

"Aha," he exclaimed, obviously frustrated.

There was a small duffel bag at the bottom of my wardrobe. He unzipped it, sat it at his feet, and began removing my dresses from their hangers. One by one, he rolled them in little balls and stuffed them into the bag.

"Why not fold them?" I asked, meeting him at the wardrobe.

"Lillian will press them when you return."

"Why make her press them? Why not fold them?"

"Please, go sit down. Let me take care of this." He waved me away.

My time at home, at my father's home, suddenly seemed like a dream. It wasn't possible that I had traveled to New York, grown up, and traveled back here to find myself. And the self that I thought I had found was hiding like a coward. She had cowered in the shadows the instant Charlie came into view.

"Where are you?" I whispered to myself.

"Did you say something?" Charlie asked, still torturing my dresses.

I simply shook my head.

"I swear, Maggie. I don't like what small town life has done to you. Take your hair for instance, I can't tell if you're styling it differently or not styling it at all."

Instinctively, my fingers went to my hair. And that's when I felt it. The self I had found, the self that had hidden, had now reappeared, poking the skin on my wrist. "Charlie?" I called him, while pulling my mother's letter from my shirtsleeve. "Would you consider staying for a while . . . just a few days? I could show you around town."

"Don't be silly. We must leave today!"

"You can have your tickets transferred. You wouldn't be out any money."

"It isn't the money, Maggie. It's the show. I have been given leave for one performance and one performance only. By leaving on this afternoon's train, I will have exactly three hours to refresh before returning to the stage. Staying here is out of the question."

"I'm sorry, but, I'm simply not prepared to leave today."

"Nonsense," he snickered. "I've practically got you packed already. You'll be prepared. Have no fear."

I rose from the bed and held my mother's letter to my chest with both hands.

"Charlie, what I meant to say, was that I am not mentally prepared."

"Mentally . . . mentally prepared?" he mocked. "Maggie, don't tell me you've finally gone and gotten a mind of your own?" He took the letter from my hands, glanced at the folded paper and, with no regard, tossed it onto the nightstand. "There's nothing here, Maggie. This place will shrivel you up and blow you away. You're nothing here. Come home where people love you and know who you really are."

"And who am I, really?" Our shoulders brushed as I moved past him. "Who does everyone think I really am? Maggie, the girl with no mind of her own? Maggie, the hired stagehand?"

Once again his grip on my arms brought Mother back to life.

"Maggie, you're out of control. I feel I don't even know you."

He released me and moved over to the window, leaning against the pane as he continued. "What is it you want? You want me to stay? Is that all this is about? Do you want me to lose my placement in the show? I am not irreplaceable, you know. And neither are you."

"Excuse me?"

"You can stay here if you want. But I am leaving on this afternoon's train. Was I so foolish to think you would want to return with me? If I didn't know you better I would think perhaps you have met someone else."

He followed my eyes to the floor, to the bed, to the window.

"My God, don't tell me you've honestly met someone. In such a short time? *Here* of all places? Why, you came here to bury your mother."

To my surprise, there were no tears waiting for their cue. There were no butterflies skipping about in my belly. To my surprise, there were no feelings at all. Had I met someone else? Had my time with John simply been the forming of a friendship? Is it possible I misread his signs? Had I only presumed to know his intentions? I turned to face myself in the mirror on my vanity. There, looking back at me was a child.

Charlie moved in behind me, his reflection placed over my shoulder.

"There is no one," I answered. "Only you."

"I'm not so certain I believe you." He placed his hands on my shoulders. "Your returning with me will put my heart at ease."

With the exception of our steps, the house was silent. Charlie carried my bags down the stairs and onto the front porch. I stood, leaning against the door frame leading into my father's study. My father and I stared at one another, at last we had found the passage to knowing the other's thoughts without speaking them aloud--a gift I had never known with my mother, and one I was sad to have only just received with my father.

He wanted to beg me to stay. Wanted to cry, and scream, and literally tie me to the chair if that's what it took. But, he also wanted me to be the adult I had become. Every parent faces this moment. The moment when they must let their child walk blindly into the face of danger, because otherwise they will never learn the lesson. They will never know what is at stake unless they are forced to choose the path on their own.

I knew in his silence, he was speaking to God. Asking Him to protect me, to give me wisdom. He was praying that he had passed enough on to me, that I would choose the right way. That I would turn back before I walked the line that once crossed, can never be uncrossed. My father prayed that day. So did I. My prayer was being answered with every silent breath my father took. The fact that he didn't cry, scream, or attempt to tie me to the chair was enough evidence to me that there was, indeed, a God.

"Shall we be off?" His words shook me--broke me from the spell I had shared with my father. Charlie kissed my cheek with confidence and crossed the room to shake my father's hand. They exchanged a courteous good-bye and Charlie kissed my cheek again as he passed by me. "I'll wait for you outside."

We stood a moment longer in silence. This was our life. We were now the husband and daughter of a deceased alcoholic. We were now a father and daughter that had learned to be friends, and now I was leaving. I wasn't being sent away. I wasn't being rescued. I was making the choice to leave. I hated myself for it. I hated God for giving me the choice. I hated Charlie for swaying my decision. I hated John for not giving me reason to stay. I hated my father for having faith in me to choose wisely.

"Delitha," he finally spoke, "What did your mother tell you?"

"To live the life I was intended to live. What did she tell you?"

"To *let* you live the life you were intended to live." He put his hands in his pockets. "I'm going to miss you."

26

Charlie and I walked hand in hand toward the train. My hand kept slipping and his insisted on tightening the grip. As we approached our entrance, I thought I heard someone call my name. I remember turning to look, but there was no one there. No one I recognized, anyway. My attention had gone back to Charlie for only a moment when I heard it again. This time my entire body turned to look.

"What is it?" he asked me.

"Nothing. I thought I heard someone call my . . ."

"Delitha, wait!"

It was then that I saw him, rushing toward me like the wind.

"Delitha, please don't leave." His speech was broken as he bent at the waist to catch his breath. Charlie took me by the arm and turned me toward him. His left eyebrow raised far above the right one.

"Please don't tell me *this* is why you don't want to leave."

All I could do was look down at my feet. My emotions were once again controlled by the child inside me. In my heart was the woman I had become; she was screaming to get out and show her face, but the little girl was strong enough to hold her back.

"Maggie, don't be serious. This man could easily be your father! He won't last past the honeymoon!" He laughed and tugged at my arm. "Come before the train leaves without us."

We took two steps toward the train, when John stood up straight, towering over Charlie.

"Delitha, don't leave me," he spoke gently, quietly, and Charlie could not resist mocking him.

"*Don't leave me, don't leave me.* Of course he doesn't want you to leave him. All old men are afraid of being alone. Can't you see? He doesn't need you, he wants you to care for him." He stepped one foot onto the train and gripped the handrail. "Now say your silly goodbyes and let's get home."

He boarded the train, confident that I would follow him; and I did, having said no good-byes. I stepped aboard backward, my eyes locked with John's. He removed his hat and with both hands he held it to his chest.

"I am old, Delitha. Your friend is right about that. But, I'm not afraid of being alone, just of being without you."

Tears began welling in my eyes. My nose began to burn and my throat constricted. My intention was to stand there, if for only a moment, just to clear my head. However, my intentions were interrupted by a heavy tap on my shoulder. "The train will be leaving soon, ma'am. You'd better take your seat."

Charlie was sitting on an aisle seat, facing me as I approached him.

"Ah, I knew you would make the right choice. The obvious choice." He stroked his hair back as he referred to himself as *the obvious choice*. I placed myself in the aisle seat facing him. I spent a few moments studying his face.

"Charlie, can I ask you something?"

"You can ask me anything, doll face." He leaned forward and rested his elbows on his knees. He smelled of cigar smoke.

"Have you ever . . . I mean do you . . ."

"Spit it out, doll face, I'm getting older by the second."

"Do you want to marry me? Do you want to make a life with me?"

He leaned back in his seat and crossed his legs. The conductor was making his last call for all aboard. Charlie uncrossed his legs and crossed them again in the other direction. At last he leaned forward again placing both feet flat on the floor. He raised his hands and turned them down pointing at his shoes. My eyes followed his and I watched as he performed a simple tap step in our tiny compartment.

"Maggie," he whispered, "I just want to dance. The dance is my life."

The train began inching away from the depot. As I rose from my seat, I pulled the ring Charlie had given me from my finger and let it slip from my hand. The violet stone blurred as it hit the floor.

"Goodbye." I whispered to him.

"Goodbye? Good heavens, where are you going?" He leaned over and looked out the window. "To him? You've got to be kidding!"

I turned and made my way to the exit, Charlie was right on my heels.

"He's not like us, Maggie. He can't make you happy."

"No, *you* are not like *us.*"

"Sir, madam, you must return to your seats," Came a voice from a man I could not see.

"Maggie, come and sit down."

I gave Charlie one last look, "My mother didn't name me Maggie," I told him. "She named me Delitha. Delitha Susan Viney Missy Leigh. That is who I am!"

Gathering my skirt, I closed my eyes and jumped back onto the platform.

Charlie leaned out from the exit. He had nothing to say and had the train come to a complete stop, I knew he wouldn't come after me. It was then I realized it was Charlie who was afraid of being alone. And it wasn't me that filled the void, it was the audience waiting for him at the theater. I was merely the hired stagehand. The pretty girl that all successful men had hanging from their arm. And he was right about one thing, I was not irreplaceable.

As the glaring sun blurred my sight, I turned to find an empty platform. I ran as fast as my feet would allow me, back through the station and onto the road out front. He was there, opening the door to his car. John was the most handsome man I had ever laid eyes on. Even then, in my mad rush to catch him, he stood me still.

John threw his hat inside the car and closed the door, moving toward me slowly.

Standing before me, with sunlight spraying around him, I saw his youth peeking through. His hair was dark and wavy, his face tight and flawless. He smiled his intoxicating smile.

"I am not the wife you once had," I told him.

"No, you certainly are not. And she was not you."

With that, with there being no more pressing words to speak, John cupped my face in his hands and kissed me. He kissed me with the vigor that only lives within a real man. Vigor I had never felt before that day.

I later learned that John had woken from a dream that morning as well. A dream where Ida and I sat side by side playing with our dolls on the floor of her kitchen. We both looked up and smiled as John entered the room, removing his hat and wiping his brow with his forearm. Ida and I stood, coming of age in an instant, our dolls becoming bouquets of fresh flowers. John and I moved toward each other as our clothing transformed into wedding attire. His home became the foyer of the church where we greeted our guests. As we moved to the end of the line, we came to a woman standing with her back to us. "Thank you for sharing this day with us," I whispered, trying for her attention. She turned and showed her tear-stained face. It was Carolyn. "Blessing's upon you both," she said. "You're happiness will be my peaceful rest."

When John awoke from this dream, he sat with Carolyn's picture until his heart felt at ease. Until he had said goodbye. He shaved, dressed in his Sunday suit, and walked over to my father's house with intentions of asking permission for my hand. My father explained the morning's events and John immediately left for the station. After I boarded the train, he had planned to return home and pack his own bags. He was certain enough of our love to travel to New York after me. That's the love I needed. That's the love I craved. That is the love the Good Lord used to pull me off that train.

My engagement to John Sunday was short. The ceremony was simple, yet beautiful. We exchanged our vows under the gazebo behind our home, where we would spend so many evenings together, talking and dreaming. My father pronounced us man and wife. Ida and Aunt Esther threw rose petals on us as we walked away. We walked away, not as two, but as one. I felt, as we walked, completely encompassed by love.

Love, I have been told, can be found in the most peculiar places. It can sneak up and take hold of you when you least expect it. When you don't even realize you need it or want it. Love is a peculiar thing. It is beautiful in its peculiarity and irresistible in its approach. It may come over you slowly like the sweet juice from an orange dripping down your chin. Or, it might rush over you like ice cold water hitting your sun-warmed face. Fast or slow, when it hits you, there's no denying it. No escaping it.

I have been blessed in my life to have experienced love. Love in all its forms. I have felt the love of the sister I never had, the best friend from my childhood. I have felt the love of a stranger, a woman who took me in and gave me a new life. I have felt a love that is often misunderstood, a love disguised by selfish needs. I have tasted this love in the shadow of a boy whose hopes and dreams were very different than my own.

Love had taken hold of John's heart and had used its powers to bring me back home. Back home to my father. Back home to a life and a fortune that had been hidden from me in my youth. Little did I know, I would also find a love I never knew existed. Love for a woman; my Mother, whose memory, had I returned to New York, would have remained in the ground. For the first time in my life, I could honestly say I had seen and felt the brilliance of the tide.

27

Several times through the years, I have been greeted with news that changed the course of my life. We can't see the future, so we can't see the changes that will come with the visit of a stranger, a letter in the mail, a telegram or by opening your heart to unexpected love. Most often, it isn't until years later that we look back and see how everything worked together to bring us to where we are. I expect more changes in my life. Change, after all, is inevitable. I did not, however, expect the change that would come from a headline that greeted me on the morning's paper.

It was only a matter of time before the effects of the stock market crash trickled to Georgia. Only the wealthy hoped to stand on solid ground. Only the ones whose family name preceded the word "fortune" seemed to have a chance of survival.

It was during this time that my father took to the road. Traveling to the camps trying to spread hope rather than panic. Trying to make sense of the chaos. Trying to give those sinking in the unforgiving sand a strong sturdy hand to hold on to. He is after all, a messenger.

He sent word that families were splitting before his very eyes. He said he would never forget the cries of the mothers handing over their children. Mothers who could offer their children nothing but the milk from their breast. And even that supply was running dry from a lack of nourishment.

He, my father, had an idea. An idea that would change everything. We would open both our homes to as many children as possible. We would love them, nourish them and educate them. We would be their home away from home. We argued over opening my father's home with him on the road. How could John and I possibly maintain two households?

"The Good Lord will provide. "My father said with confidence.

My father spread the word throughout the camps, offering our help with any children that needed care. He was to arrive on a Wednesday morning. He and twenty-five children. John and I spent that morning nervously pacing the halls of our home. We passed each other with blank stares, each of us wondering what we had gotten ourselves into.

We both heard it. A knock at the door. We both stopped and jerked our heads toward the sound. I gently squeezed John's arm as I pushed past him. At the door, I took in a deep breath before reaching for the handle. Change is inevitable. Change was waiting for me on the other side of the door.

My father stood, smiling proudly, surrounded by children of all ages. But, not just children.

"You'll never believe this, Dell." My father said, with a voice shaking with excitement. Next to my father stood Henry, Eloise and a beautiful little girl I could only assume was Emiline. Henry stood holding his hat to his chest, smiling from ear to ear.

"We heard you needed help." Eloise bellowed, "so we came a runnin'."

That first night, after the last cheek had been kissed and covers tucked tight, I found John outside on the front porch, leaning on the railing. Leaning, not out of exhaustion, but in appreciation. In admiration. This home, our home, was serving its purpose. John had an unmistakable joy in his heart. A joy, he said, that comes from doing what you were meant to do. I understood that joy. I felt it. I realized it. I too, was doing what I was meant to do. I was meant to follow in the footsteps of the two women who molded me into the woman I am today. I was meant to be an innkeeper. I was meant to be a rescuer.

While John enjoyed a moment of calm on the front porch, I retreated to my refuge; my haven. I sat under Ol' Willy for only a moment before I realized this spot would soon be found out. Ol' Willy would soon be treasured by other boys and girls. I patted his trunk. I was excited to share him; to share more of my heart.

From under Ol' Willy's protective branches, I turned and looked at my father's house. I could picture my mother stepping out onto the back porch; stealing a moment of fresh air. My father would soon join her and stand at her back wrapping his arms around her waist. They both wore smiles. It was in that memory that I saw what I had failed to see as a child. That day, I saw the love in my mother's heart. I felt that love and it became clear to me that my mother could not have lived the life that she did, had her heart been as cold as

I had thought it to be. I realized something else that day. Something that Ida had said to me many years before. She had placed her hand over my heart and said that I would find the person I had been looking for in New York. But, she was wrong. I found myself, that person I had been looking for, right here in Georgia.

Each day has brought new struggles, new joys. Each day that passes sends older children back to work the fields and brings younger ones in to escape the madness. Each knock at the door brings a new story to our home; brings new light and hope to a child. It was the call I received this morning that has allowed me to recount my life. To examine all the details that have made me who I am, brought me to where I am.

"Mr. Talbot, from the "Chronicle", the one who invited you all to my home, said that the hope we are giving these children has traveled far beyond the borders of Georgia. He said he wanted to help spread the word, spread the hope. Spread the notion for others to open their homes and their hearts and work as an extended family to get through this time."

I am surrounded by cameras and men in dark suits. They scribble on small white paper as I speak. They have come here today, curious of my life. Of my homes, my husband, Henry, Eloise, Emiline, and the children we serve. They have traveled here to become acquainted with the life of the innkeeper, Sister Sunday. Yet, they will leave here most acquainted with a young girl named Delitha. Delitha Susan Viney Missy Leigh.

"My life as Sister Sunday," I tell them, "has only just begun."

ABOUT THE AUTHOR

Beth Ann Baus has spent most of her adult life counseling women who have experienced varying degrees of abuse. It's no surprise that the horrors of abuse and the path to healing are main themes in her writing. Beth was raised in Tennessee but now makes her home in Ohio with her husband and two sons.

28279444R00119

Made in the USA
Lexington, KY
12 January 2019